MW00413190

TALES FOR GULLIBLE CHILDREN

BY

LAURA WATKINS

Copyright © 2019 by Laura Watkins

All rights reserved. No part of this book may be used or reproduced by any means, graphic, electronic, or mechanical, including photocopying, recording, taping, or by any information storage retrieval system, without the written permission of the publisher except in the case of brief quotations embodied in critical articles and reviews.

DEDICATION

For Joe, who taught me to lie to children.

*"Now, believe it or not, and I've been known to lie,
this here is a true story."*

--Ren and Stimpy

"Big House Blues"

TABLE OF CONTENTS

Uncle Joey and the Secret of Fire

This is a story from the early 1990s, children, long before you were born. It was a dark and miserable time. There were no iPads, our telephones were stuck to the walls of our houses, and all of our games were on boards and all our books were on paper. Yes, like you flush down the toilet. SpongeBob had not even been thought of; instead, we watched Ren and Stimpy, featuring a superhero named Powdered Toast Man and a law enforcement agency called the Royal Canadian Kilted Yaksmen. No, really.

But the worst part of the early nineties, children, was your Uncle Joey's mullet. Have you ever seen a mullet? It was a hairstyle that seemed to come from the depths of Hell itself: short and spiky on the top, long and greasy in the back. Uncle Joey's, which he wore with polo shirts and thick aviator-framed glasses, was especially terrible. He looked like a less-hip Jeffrey Dahmer.

Where was I? Oh yes, the nineties. In the nineties, as you may know, fire had not yet been discovered; people ate nothing but cold cereal and, on special occasions, raw hot dogs. These were not very good, but there was nothing else, so people just sucked it up.

Now, back in those ancient days, it was the custom in Missoula to mark the summer equinox with a great festival, the climax of which was a footrace all around the town. The winner would be covered in glory, and would win the lion's share of the raw hot dogs at that night's feast. Your Uncle Joey, being a gangly fellow and fleet of foot, had entered the race, and was much favored to win. Even the gods on Mount Olympus, which, contrary to popular belief, is not in Greece but in the Rockies, bet amongst themselves on the outcome, and by the week of the race, you could not even get two to one on Joey.

What your Uncle Joey did not know, however, was that Bridger, a chubby, bearded young man from Joe's school, had set his eyes on the crates of raw hot dogs being stacked in the town square, and he had resolved to win both the race and the hot dogs for himself. The night before the race, tiptoeing and cackling softly, Bridger snuck out to the race course and, a hundred yards or so before the finish line, began to dig a hole.

The moon was the only witness to Bridger's evil deed. Beginning in the center of the path, he dug and dug, down and down, until finally, sweating and exhausted, he saw magma bubble up under his shovel, and he knew that he had reached the earth's core. He scrambled up and out of the hole, giggling, and proceeded to disguise his handiwork with some branches and leaves.

"Ha ha!" he chortled. "I'll slip off the course and hide in those trees over there to wait. When Joe comes along, he'll think he's won, and he won't be paying attention to where he steps. He'll fall in the hole and never be seen again, and I'll run across the finish line myself. Then all those beautiful hot dogs will be MINE!" Slinging his shovel across his back, Bridger scuttled off back to his mom's basement, washed his hands, and fell into a sinister sleep.

Now Zeus, the king of the gods, suffered from insomnia, and he was up late on Mount Olympus watching infomercials when his eye happened to catch what the wicked Bridger was doing. "Ho ho!" he said to himself. "Bridger is going at forty to one for tomorrow's race, with no takers. I'll bet on him and clean up like a rock star!" He immediately rang Big Eddie, the bookie of the gods, and put his entire paycheck on Bridger at forty to one. Then he also went to sleep, dreaming of the vintage Camaro he would buy, and how it would finally shut up Apollo, who thought he was such hot shit with his chariot of fire.

The next day dawned, bright and peach-colored, and the contestants took their places at the starting line. "You look tired, Bridger," said Uncle Joey.

"Yes, I was up all night digging a hole to the earth's core," replied Bridger.

"What was that?" said Uncle Joey, who had been tying his shoe.

"I mean, I was up all night, hoping for your victory," said Bridger, thinking fast.

"Hey, thanks, man," said Uncle Joey.

"Nice save," said Bridger.

"What?" said Uncle Joey.

"Never mind," said Bridger. "I didn't mean to say that part out loud."

"Oh, OK," said Uncle Joey, bemused. The contestants lined up. As the starting gun cracked, Uncle Joey took off like a deer strapped to the hood of a Chevy, followed, far behind, by a trundling, panting Bridger. As soon as they were out of sight of the starting area, however, Bridger veered off into the woods. He cut across town, to a spot near the finish line where he had stashed a backpack full of adult beverages and naughty magazines. There, he waited.

He didn't have to wait long. Striding manfully, barely puffing, Uncle Joey burst out of the forest and headed straight for Bridger's trap. There was nobody else in sight. On Olympus, the gods were watching, leaning over the miniature version of Missoula on the floor of their rec room. Zeus smirked and cast a sideways glance at Apollo.

Just as Bridger had planned, Uncle Joey's foot broke through the branches concealing the hole, and with a loud cry, he vanished from sight. Zeus hooted with glee. Bridger rolled up his magazine, stuffed it into his back pocket, and began to jog, preparing to cross the finish line himself. He smiled in his beard, for soon the hot dogs would be his, all his.

Then, an astonishing thing happened.

"*AAAAAAAAAAAAAAA!*" Uncle Joey shot out of the hole like the cork out of a champagne bottle. His mullet, acting like an ugly wing, had caught the updraft of warm air off the pit of magma, and lifted him to safety. He touched down just short of the finish line, and daintily stepped across. He had won! Bridger, still twenty yards behind, stared, open-mouthed.

In the town square, people were cheering and shouting Uncle Joey's name. On Olympus, Big Eddie in his pinstriped suit was paying out modest sums to those who had bet on Uncle Joey, but he gave nothing to Zeus. "Better luck next time, big fella," he said to the dejected god, as, below, the townspeople led Uncle Joey to the victor's podium, which they had fashioned out of hot dog crates. They festooned him with garlands and a crown and placed him on the highest crate, chanting all the while "JOE-Y! JOE-Y!" Bridger skulked along behind the procession, scowling fiercely. He would have those hot dogs yet, by hook or by crook.

Up on Olympus, Zeus paced in despair, clutching at his curly head. How was he going to explain this to his wife? A whole paycheck lost, and just when the heater was going on the fritz and his truck needed new tires! Distraught, Zeus picked up a lightning bolt that was lying nearby and flung it down the mountain at Joe. At that exact moment, however, the wicked, revenge-seeking Bridger hurled himself at Joe, knocking him down and preparing to beat him to death with a naughty magazine. The lightning bolt missed Joe by inches, setting the crates of hot dogs ablaze.

"Thanks, buddy," said Uncle Joey, pinned to the pavement by Bridger's great bulk. "You saved me."

"Prepare to die!" Bridger was about to say, when he paused, arrested by the most delicious aroma wafting across the square. The hot dogs in the burning crates were cooking, and people were using sticks to fish them out and dunk them in ketchup.

The mayor tasted one, tentatively. "Why, these are scrumptious!" he declared, taking another bite. "Quickly, save some fire in a bag, so that we can use it later! Young Joe and Bridger have saved us from raw hot dogs!" The people began to cheer again, and hoisted Joe and Bridger on their shoulders. "JOE-Y! JOE-Y!" they chanted. "BRIDG-ER! BRIDG-ER!"

On Olympus, Zeus' jaw hung open. First a lost paycheck, and now the secret of fire had been stolen by a pair of upstart boys from Missoula! As soon as this got around, even the riffraff would be eating cooked food, and before you knew it, there would be no way to tell the mortals from the gods. Zeus could just hear Apollo now, sneering, "Oh, you know, being an Olympian used to mean something. Until *someone* was careless and lost the fire." He buried his face in his hands.

Down the mountain in Missoula, the chanting crowd was doing laps of the town square. "Dude, your mullet!" called Bridger, double-fisting a pair of charred hot dogs as he rode the shoulders of two burly townspeople. "The lightning must have burned it off!"

Joe touched the singed ends of his now-shortened hair. "Probably for the best," he called back. "I always thought it looked kind of creepy."

"Yeah, I hate you way less without it. Here, catch! These are really good!" Bridger pitched one of his hot dogs across.

Joe gnawed and swallowed. "You're right, these are great! Bet they'd be even better with mustard!" As the crowd milled back towards the festival grounds, they deposited Joe and Bridger back beside the blazing hot dog crates. The two boys grinned shyly at each other. And everyone was happy.

And that, children, is the story of how your Uncle Joey stole fire from the gods. Later on, of course, someone else invented matches, and everyone was less impressed, but at the time, it was a pretty big deal. Oh, and it's also how he met his best friend.

THE END

How Uncle Joey Cheated the Devil

This story is from the mid-1990s, children, after your Uncle Joey stole the secret of fire from the gods and had his mullet singed off by a lightning bolt hurled by Zeus, but before he vanquished the dragon and rescued the maiden fair (which is another story altogether).

It was a couple of weeks before Christmas, and the only thing in the world that Uncle Joey wanted was a Super Rex Mighty Turbo Ultra RC Racer, one of the finest remote control trucks ever to cruise the streets and parking lots of Missoula. It could spin, it could climb, and it came with dual-action aimable pellet cannons. Unfortunately, it also came with a hefty price tag.

Uncle Joey didn't get a very big allowance, so he couldn't afford to buy a Super Rex Mighty Turbo Ultra RC Racer, but that didn't stop him from dreaming. Every day on his way home from school, he'd stop in front of the big window of the neighborhood toy shop and look at the Super Rex, gleaming in its black and silver trim on a pedestal in the middle of the display. The chrome buttons and antenna of the remote seemed to call Uncle Joey's name, and he would sigh, imagining himself on the playground, popping wheelies and spinning donuts as his classmates groaned with envy. Then, heavy-hearted, he would turn away, and plod home to his chores.

One day, he lingered a little longer than usual in front of the toy shop. As he prepared to pull himself away, though, he felt a hand settle on his shoulder. "Nice car," a deep, cultured voice drawled. "A bit expensive, though."

Joey turned to look. The hand was pale, hairless, and smooth, with long, white, well-manicured nails. It disappeared into the sleeve of a thick wool coat, and as Joey's eyes traveled upward, he took in the wearer's neat silk scarf, fastened with a gold and ruby pin, and his gleaming black top hat. The man smiled a smile that contained a few too many teeth. "Do you suppose that Santa Claus will bring it to you for Christmas, little boy?"

Uncle Joey shook his head, unable to break the stranger's gaze. "No. My dad says toys like that are for kids who are a lot better behaved than me."

"Mmm. On the naughty list, are you?" The stranger sighed, exhaling the scent of dead flowers. "Ah, well. Perhaps you can have one later, when you have a job of your own. Of course, at that point, you won't have any time to play with it." His eyes slid sideways, slyly. "Unless…"

"Unless what?" Joey felt himself oddly mesmerized, fascinated by the stranger's manner.

"It's possible that I may have access to a limited supply of complimentary Super Rex Racers, to be distributed to the right little boys." He crooked his finger, and with a whir, a shiny new Super Rex zipped out of a nearby alley and parked obediently at his feet. "Naughtiness is no obstacle, though there is a bit of paperwork to be done. And of course, a small processing fee."

Joey frowned. "How much?" He only had a few dollars in his piggy bank.

"Just one."

"One dollar?"

"One soul." The stranger smiled more broadly, withdrawing a rolled parchment from his sleeve. "Payable on demise, of course. Play now, and pay later." A fountain pen appeared in his right hand. "All you have to do is make your mark on the line. Two strokes of the pen, and it's yours."

Uncle Joey stared up into the stranger's face. With a creeping dread, he took in the yellow eyes glowing like coals, the slit pupils narrowing with glee. Tendrils of smoke wreathed from the black fur collar of the stranger's coat, forming a halo around his head. Uncle Joey realized that he was looking at the devil.

"Get AWAY!" he cried, slapping the pen out of the stranger's hand. He turned and fled down the block, and he didn't stop until he got to his friend Bridger's house. Leaning against the side of the house, he panted, listening for the footsteps of the pursuing devil. There was nothing.

By and by, however, his straining ears picked up a familiar whir. Joey crept slowly towards the corner of the house. "Bridger?" he called softly.

"Hey, dude." Bridger's voice returned. "Check it out."

Somewhat reassured, Joey put his head around the corner. Bridger was parked on the steps of the back porch. In his hands was a boxy chrome remote control with a long antenna. On the concrete pad in front of him, a black and silver Super Rex Racer zoomed through a homemade obstacle course, executing slaloms and jumps with ease.

"Hey!" Uncle Joey started forward, surprised. "I thought your mom said you'd get a Super Rex after your ski vacation in Hell."

"It's not from Mom." Bridger put the Super Rex up on one wheel and made it pirouette. "Some guy down by the toy store is giving them away for free."

Uncle Joey gulped. "Tall guy, black coat? Looks kind of evil?"

"That's the guy. You should go see him, I'll bet he has some more."

"And you didn't have to do anything at all?" Uncle Joey was waiting for Bridger to realize what had happened. It looked like being a long wait.

"I had to fill out a paper. Some kind of survey or something."

Joey couldn't take it any longer. "Bridger, that wasn't a survey, it was a contract! You just sold your soul to the devil!"

Bridger made the Super Rex bounce like an excited puppy. "Worth it."

"But—"

Uncle Joey didn't have time to finish his sentence. With a whoosh of blue flame, the devil materialized in the middle of Bridger's backyard. He stepped forward out of a cloud of brimstone smoke, flicking ash from his cuffs. "Good afternoon, Joey. Nice to see you again. Bridger." His face creased with pleasure. "I've come to collect on your debt."

"What?" gasped Uncle Joey. "I thought Bridger got to keep his soul until he died."

"That is the standard agreement, yes. However, your friend elected to purchase several of the optional upgrades, which of course shortens the term of the contract.

Joey turned to Bridger. "Optional upgrades?"

"Neutrino cannon. Totally cool." Bridger fiddled with the controls. "I think it's this button." A blast of green light flashed out from the Super Rex, blowing a hole in the fence and vaporizing the neighbor's poodle.

Joey turned back to the devil. "What will happen to Bridger without his soul?"

The devil shrugged. "Not my problem, really. Perhaps he'll move to San Diego and open a yoga studio."

"NO!" Joe picked up a Nerf bat that had been lying nearby and squared up against the devil. "Bridger is MY friend and he will NOT go to San Diego!"

The devil laughed with a sound like a mine caving in. "It's not up to you, little boy. A bargain is a bargain." With a flick of his wrist, he sent Joey spinning and tumbling into the garbage cans stacked by the fence. "Now, then," he said, returning his attention to Bridger. "Just hold still, will you? This will only hurt a little." An enormous steel syringe with a needle like a harpoon appeared in his hands.

"Wait!" gasped Uncle Joey. He struggled up out of the pile of trash. "Double or nothing?"

The devil looked quizzical. "I beg your pardon?"

"Double or nothing." Joey took a deep breath. "We play a game. If you win, you can have Bridger's soul, and mine too. If I win, you have to leave, and Bridger keeps his soul."

"A game!" The devil looked delighted. "I'll admit, I do have a weakness for gambling. Very well, I accept." He held out his cold hand, and after a moment's hesitation, Joey took it and shook it. "Now, what shall it be? Chess? A single hand of poker?"

Joey dipped his hand into his pocket. "Something a little more casual."

The devil frowned. "Not Battleship, surely? How cliché."

"No." Joey opened his hand, displaying a small, crocheted blob. "Hacky sack."

"Hacky sack? How quaint. How do you play?" the devil said with a smirk.

"Like this." Uncle Joey began to kick the hacky sack, batting it with his feet. "The only rule is that it can't touch the ground." He kicked it extra hard, flipping it through the air to the devil. "Here, you try."

The devil kicked for the hacky sack, but as he did so, his shoe flew off, revealing a cloven hoof, which missed entirely, and the hacky sack plopped to the ground. "Heh heh," he chuckled, masking his embarrassment. "That was just practice. This one is the first one that counts." He kicked again with his other foot, but the second shoe did not stay on any better, and the devil stood there in his bare hooves, trying vainly to get the hacky sack in the air.

"No, no, like this." Joe took the hacky sack, and began to hop in circles around the devil, tossing it from foot to foot. "It's easy."

The devil tried again, but no matter what he did, his cloven hooves could not manage to get the hacky sack up for more than one bounce. One flip went wild, but Joey neatly corralled it. "What's the matter, devil? Stoners can do this all day long." Aiming a kick, he bounced the hacky sack off the devil's forehead. The devil turned red, then purple. Bridger, still sitting on the porch steps, giggled.

The devil boiled over. "Ohhhhhhh, FUCK IT!" he cried. "Keep your stupid soul! See if I care!" The parchment with Bridger's signature hovered in the air, then burst into flames. "Bunch of loser hicks! I will never set foot in Missoula again!" screamed the devil, and with that, he vanished in a clap of blue fire and a smell of burning ozone.

There was a minute of silence as the smoke of the devil's departure slowly dissipated. "Whoa," said Joey.

"Hey," said Bridger. "He took the Super Rex with him."

"Shut the hell up, Bridger," said Uncle Joey.

"OK," agreed Bridger. "Want to play hacky sack?"

THE END

How Uncle Joey Vanquished the Dragon and Rescued the Maiden Fair

This story, children, takes place a few years after the earlier ones. Your Uncle Joey was still living in Missoula, but it was not a happy time for him: Bridger, having over time grown to be Joey's closest friend, had suddenly all but abandoned him.

The problem was an ancient one, but none the less painful: a girl. This particular girl was a fancy chick called Lady Tara of Minnesota, and Bridger spent nearly all his time hanging around her, drinking beer and playing video games. (This last part was pretty normal for Bridger, actually; it was the hanging around with Tara that Joey objected to. Or rather, hanging around with Tara and NOT Joey.)

One day, Joe decided that enough was enough. He went over to Bridger's house. Bridger was parked on the couch in his underwear, and Lady Tara was in the kitchen, making crepes. "Bridger, what the hell?" Joe began as he entered the living room.

"Huh?" replied Bridger.

"We never get to hang out just the two of us anymore," said Joey. "It's always 'Tara can't make it that night' or 'Only if Tara is free.'"

"Hey," said Bridger, "I love Tara. She feeds me and pets me and doesn't get mad when I come home at 3 am on two flat tires with a bag full of thirty ham and cheese sandwiches." Bridger rummaged in the bowl of Cheetos he had balanced on his belly. "And besides," he continued, "what are *you* complaining for? Whenever we do go out together, she always drives us home, no matter how wasted we are." From the kitchen, Tara rolled her eyes.

Joey pouted. "But when you guys go on date nights, I'm all by myself. What am I gonna do, hang out with Dave in Dave's mom's basement? Come on."

Bridger slapped Joey's shoulder. "Joey, my boy, you're trying to solve the wrong problem. Instead of complaining about Tara, you should be sprucing yourself up and looking for your own fair maiden."

"Bridger, I know all the maidens in Missoula, and none of them are what you'd call fair. Plus, most of them have slapped me," Joey pointed out.

"Hm," grunted Bridger. "Good point. We'll have to look elsewhere." He furrowed his brow in thought. "Let's see. We'll probably want to head west, since east of Missoula is mostly grasslands and bison. Maybe to a city, because there'll be better food than in a small town. You'll want a nice restaurant to take the fair maiden to, once you've found her. I know!" Bridger stood up, elegantly picking out his wedgie and brushing the Cheeto dust from his chest hair. "Tara, honey, we're going to Portland!"

"That's great, babe." Tara appeared in the kitchen doorway, wiping her hands on a towel. "For how long?"

"As long as it takes to find a fair maiden for Joey," said Bridger, looking behind the sofa. "By the way, have you seen my pants?"

"They're in the laundry basket. I washed them."

Bridger goggled. "Pants can be washed?"

Tara sighed. "OK. Portland is a long ways away. I'd better fix a bag to take with you." She disappeared up the stairs. A second later, Bridger's pants came flying down.

"I'm telling you, you're not going to regret this, Joey," said Bridger, picking up the pants. "Believe me, I know what I'm talking about."

"Zipper goes in the front, Bridger," Joey reminded him.

"Oh yeah. Thanks," said Bridger, reversing the pants as Tara came back downstairs.

She held out a zipped duffel bag. "Here you go. Some clean underwear and snacks for the road. Oh, and this." In her other hand, she held out a long, thick wooden staff. "My dad's walking stick. It's good for long travels."

"Thanks, Tara," said Joey, touched.

"You'd better get going," she said. "There's a lot of ground between here and Portland."

Bridger kissed her goodbye, and they went outside to where Joe's dad's Suburban was parked. "Why'd we need the walking stick, again?" asked Bridger.

"I dunno, but it seemed rude not to take it. Put it in the back with the bag," said Joey. Bridger did, then they both climbed in, and they were off.

They traveled and traveled, through mountains and valleys. They saw Indian casinos and cattle farms, truck stops and souvenir stands. Not a single fair maiden. Finally, on the third day, they came to a bridge, on which was parked a tiny blue car with a very skinny man inside, wearing thick-framed glasses and a Dandy Warhols T-shirt. Joey pulled up alongside and rolled down his window. "Excuse me," he called. "Is this the way to Portland?"

The skinny man curled his lip. "I hope you don't think you're bringing that…thing into town," he said.

"What thing?" said Bridger.

The man tipped his head at the Suburban. "That. You can't bring that into Portland."

26

"SUVs are illegal in Portland?" Joey was incredulous.

"Well, no…" the man sniffed. "But they ought to be. Hybrids are so much better, don't you think? Cleaner. And quieter. And nicer looking."

"OK! Well, nice talking to you, but we have to be going on our way." Joey reversed and prepared to drive around the tiny car.

"Oh no, you don't!" cried the skinny man. With a squeal of tires, he slammed the little car backwards at an angle across the bridge, blocking both lanes. "You'll have to get past my Prius first!"

Joey ducked back inside the car. "Bridger, what's happening here?"

"It's a hipster," said Bridger. "We must be getting close to Portland."

"OK, well, how do I get past him?"

"Just run over him. You'll barely feel the bump."

"No, I can't do that. He'll get snagged and mess up my chassis. Let me think a minute." Joey leaned his forehead on the steering wheel, trying to think of everything he knew about hipsters. "OK, I have a plan. Here's what we're going to do."

A moment later, Joey opened the door of the Suburban and ambled up to the bridge railing, as if stretching his legs. He rolled his neck from side to side, taking in the view. Then, suddenly he stiffened, looking at something in the distance. He pointed off, away down the river. "Bridger, look here! Some guy is on the bank, adding fluoride to the city water supply!"

"WHAT!" screamed the hipster, leaping out of his Prius and rushing to the railing. "They can't do that! Fluoride should be a personal choice! It probably causes autis— aaaaaack!" With an audible whomp, Bridger brought down a pair of his underwear over the hipster's head, enshrouding his face. The hipster thrashed and gagged, but it was no use, and in a few moments, he lay still, overcome by the fumes.

"Good work, Bridger," said Joey. "Now help me move the Prius."

They both went to the Prius and slowly shoved it off to the side. "These are heavier than they look," panted Bridger.

"Two impulsion systems," gasped Joey, giving a final heave. "With both a gas engine and an electric motor, they're deceptively hefty. OK, that's done it. Let's go." They climbed back into the Suburban and continued on their way.

It wasn't long, however, before Bridger tugged at Joey's sleeve. "I'm hungry."

"Eat some of the snacks Tara packed for you."

"I did." Bridger displayed the bag, now empty except for some wrappers, plastic bags, and the much-licked shiny lid of a tin can.

Joey groaned. "All right. We'll stop at this place coming up on the left here." He pulled the Suburban over at a small, brightly painted building by the side of the road. He and Bridger jumped out and went inside.

"Greetings, travelers!" called a cheery voice as they entered. "What can I get started for you?" The voice belonged to a dapper-looking young man, even skinnier than the first, wearing an immaculate flannel shirt, suspenders, and elaborately waxed mustachios. He stood behind a deli counter, wiping it down with a rag.

Bridger's eyes lit up. "I'll take a roast beef and cheese sandwich, please."

"On white? Stone-milled wheat? Organic wheat? Steel-cut wheat? Sprouted rye? French roll? Ciabatta?"

"Rye would be fi–"

The man's eyes glazed over. "Free range beef? Wagyu? Kobe?" he droned, obviously stuck on a loop.

Joe leaned over to Bridger. "Another hipster?"

"Looks that way."

"What do we do?"

"Hang on. I have an idea." Bridger rummaged among the wrappers in his bag and came up with the tin can lid. "We'll use this to reflect the sun's rays into his eyes and blind him. Then we can grab some sandwiches and run."

"Bridger, what sun? It's been cloudy for days."

"You got a better idea?" Joey shook his head. "That's what I thought. Stand aside and let me work." He sidled towards the hipster, who was still droning about asiago and aged cheddar. At the critical moment, whenever that was, he whipped up the can lid. "A-HA!"

The hipster's eyes widened. His jaw dropped. He stared. Slowly, breathily, he sighed. "It's so…beautiful."

Joey edged around to see from the hipster's point of view. "Oh," he said, getting it suddenly. "He's looking at his own reflection, Bridger. Hold it there for a few minutes, and I'll make us some sandwiches."

"Can do."

Joey stepped behind the counter, gathering bread, meat, and cheese from the vast array. Within minutes, he had the bag refilled with sandwiches, organic truffle chips, and handcrafted sodas. Gently, Bridger guided the hipster's hand up to hold the can lid in place. The hipster brought it closer to his face, breath misting the surface. "My precious,'" he crooned.

Joey and Bridger hurried out the door, tossing the bag back into the Suburban. As they pulled away, Bridger said, "You know, that guy might starve to death before he looks away."

"Not my problem," said Joey, hunched over the wheel. "We're almost to Portland."

They drove and drove. Suddenly, Joey hit the brakes. There in the road ahead of them was another man, even skinnier than the first two, waving at them with a clipboard. "I'm collecting signatures for an important community initiative! Do you have a moment?" he cried.

"Another hipster," said Joey. "I'll handle it." Reaching into the back, he pulled out the walking stick Tara had given them. He hopped out of the Suburban, strolled up to the third hipster, and commenced to beat him mercilessly with the stick. The clipboard went flying, along with the hipster's stupid flat cloth cap. Finally, the hipster lay still in the road.

"Dude," said Bridger, climbing out of the Suburban. "I think he might be dead."

"And?" said Joey. Bridger shrugged. Joey handed Bridger the stick. "It's getting dark. I'm going up this side road to look for shelter. You stay here with the car, and if he moves, whack him again." He reached into the Suburban and pulled a sandwich out of the bag. "I'll take dinner with me. Be back soon." Stuffing the sandwich into his pocket, he set off uphill.

It seemed as though he climbed for hours through the waning light in the pine forest. The road led up and up, before it finally leveled off in a small clearing. There, set into the side of the hill, appeared to be the entrance to a small cave. Joe decided to investigate.

Inside, the cave was warm and dank, and slightly smelly. The air vibrated slightly, as if someone were snoring. Piles of cloth lay everywhere. Joe turned in the middle of the large chamber, and that's when he saw the dragon.

It was huge, red-faced, with glinting green eyes like chips of broken bottle glass. A mane of wiry copper and purple hair flowed from the back of its head, but what Joe noticed was the teeth. White and sharp, they glittered in the half light as it skinned back its lips and howled. The dragon lunged.

Instinctively, Joe backpedaled, but the dragon followed. He dodged, trying to keep stalactites between his body and the teeth. He groped in his pocket, hoping to find a knife, a flashlight, anything, but his hand only closed on a paper-wrapped square. As the open-mawed dragon roared and lunged again, Joe shrieked and flung the sandwich, then dropped to the ground and covered his head.

Silence. Well, not quite silence. Through the musty air came a soft sound. *Snarf, snarf snarf.* Joe peeked between his fingers.

The dragon was gone. Instead, on a cushion in a corner, there sat a young woman, crosslegged, with purple-streaked red hair. She was eating Joey's sandwich. "Mmmf," she said, by way of greeting.

Slowly, Joe uncurled. "Hi," he said.

"Mmf," said the young woman again. She swallowed the last of the sandwich, licking her fingers daintily. "Mmm. Roast beef and cheese. My favorite." She rose from her cushion and walked over to Joey, holding out a hand. "Sorry about that. I can be kind of a beast when I'm hungry. I'll get you another sandwich, though."

Tentatively, Joey took the outstretched hand and let himself be helped to his feet. "I'm Joe," he said.

"Laura," replied the woman. "Nice to meet you. I'm new here in town, so I don't know many people yet." She gazed at Joey appreciatively. "So I'm glad you showed up."

Joey gazed back. "Me too." He took a deep breath. "Are you still hungry? I know a little deli not far from here that has great free sandwiches."

"You had me at free sandwiches." Laura slipped her arm into Joe's. "C'mon, less standing, more sandwiches." They began to walk, but at the entrance to the cave, she stopped. "Just one thing, before we go too far. Tell me…" She looked into Joey's eyes. "Do you like to shoot guns?"

Joey laughed. "Baby, I'm from Montana. I've been shooting guns since I was six years old."

Laura broke into a wide grin. "Very well. This date can continue." Arm in arm, they ambled down the trail in the sunset light.

And they lived happily ever after.

THE END

Joe and the Flathead Lake Monster

This story, children, is from not so very long ago and not so very far away. In fact, it happened just this summer, on the shores of Flathead Lake, less than a day away from the house where you live. Just imagine the scene, children: it was a beautiful summer day, and the scent of barbecuing ribs wafted on the air. The sun beamed down gently from a sky as blue as a robin's egg, while the breeze ruffled the hair of your Uncle Joey and Aunt Laura and their friends Bridger and Tara, as they stood at the end of a wooden dock, laughing at their family friend Justin, who was failing to launch his boat.

You see, children, Justin was an idiot. He could not do one single thing right. He could not even eat a sandwich like a reasonable person (he always let the filling drop everywhere), and here he was, trying to launch an expensive fishing boat. First, as he was backing down the ramp, he hit the brakes too hard, causing the boat to shoot backwards off the trailer and onto the concrete. Then, he tried to gun it backwards and scoot the boat back onto the trailer, but he only succeeded in scraping it along the ramp, tipping it and filling it with water. It drifted a bit, gliding out over a deepwater channel, and began to sink, bubbling merrily all the way.

Joey rolled on the dock, howling; Bridger slapped his thigh, and Tara wiped her eyes. It was the funniest thing they'd ever seen, at least since the time Justin rolled his RV. Justin himself stood befuddled, watching the boat as it settled lower and lower in the clear blue lake. Laura hopped up on one of the dock pylons, giggling, and began to play a jaunty tune on her banjo, Matilda.

Suddenly, there was a scream and a massive splash, and Laura was not there anymore. Where she had been standing, there was only the wet stain of what appeared to be a giant, reptilian footprint, drying in the sunshine. The water swirled with bubbles, rapidly dissipating. Tara pointed numbly. "It...it took her. It just grabbed her and dived. Some kind of creature..."

Joe didn't stop to ask questions. "Come on, Bridger!" he cried, running to the end of the dock and leaping towards the shadow of Justin's submerged boat. "We have to save Laura!" Bridger followed without hesitation, jumping in and dogpaddling after Joe.

"Hey, stop!" yelled Justin, wading into the shallows and thrashing after Bridger. "That's MY boat!" He also dived at the shadow where Joe and Bridger had disappeared beneath the waves.

Underwater, Joe had located the boat's ignition and started it up, the propeller turning slowly at first, and then faster and faster as he gave the engine more juice. Soon the boat was cruising under the water, every bit as fast as it would have on the surface. Yes, of course that's possible, children. What, suddenly you know everything? Be quiet and listen to the story.

Joe, Bridger, and Justin clung to the boat's rails as it went down, down, down, following the bubble trail that seemed to lead ever farther into the depths. They followed until they thought their lungs would burst and their ears would rupture from the pressure, into the deep, dark, silent blue. Then, from above came a flash of red-gold light, then another. Joe let go of the boat and swam upwards towards the light, the others close behind.

Their heads broke the surface, and they gasped for air as their eyes adjusted to the darkness. They were in a pool in the center of a huge, dank cave. Water dripped from the ceiling, and the rocks were slick with algae as they hauled themselves out onto the floor. The walls were riddled with niches and blind tunnels, but the red glow that illuminated the cave seemed to be emanating from one giant tunnel in the far wall, from which rushed drafts of hot, curiously dry air.

The cave itself was strewn with small, draggled objects, some lying in heaps, others leaning against the walls. Joe picked one up and wiped it against his shorts. He frowned, straightening scraps of cloth and swirls of blond hair. "Is this a doll?" Sure enough, the place was littered with dolls–big ones, little ones, Barbies and American Girls. Joe turned to the others. "What the hell does it mean? Where's Laura?"

"Joe, don't move. Don't move a muscle," Bridger whispered. From the alcove behind Joe came a faint susurration, the sliding of scales on granite. In the shadows, a tectonic shifting movement as something gray and muscular and very, very large stretched, rolled over, and lay still again. "It's the Flathead Lake Monster," breathed Bridger. "We have to get out of here."

Of course you have heard of the Flathead Lake Monster, children. Enormous in size, it resembles a large Nile monitor lizard: blunt, oblong head with forked tongue, powerful shoulders and long, muscular body, whiplike tail. Like the monitor, its bite is said to be poisonous due to bacteria it carries in its mouth; unlike the monitor, its heavily clawed feet are webbed, the better to swim in the depths of the lake. Rarely spotted, it is rumored to be extremely dangerous, being blamed in the disappearance of dozens of pets, several campers, and at least one fighter jet. And it was sleeping lightly, less than twenty feet behind your Uncle Joey.

"Joe, stay calm," whispered Bridger. "Just do exactly as I say, and we'll get out of here OK. Take one step towards me, very slowly. Don't make a sound."

Justin farted.

Behind Joe, two luminous green eyes snapped open, rising in height as the monster rolled to its feet. The beast chuffled in surprise, then, noticing the intruders, it uncoiled its full fifty-foot length and let out a horrible screaming roar. As it lowered its head to charge, the boys turned and fled towards the large, glowing tunnel. They could feel its awful wet breath on their backs as it shrieked again, and Justin stumbled over his own feet and fell headlong into a puddle. "GUYS!" he screamed, reaching out for Joe and Bridger's receding forms.

"We know, it's too late for you, save ourselves!" yelled Joe over his shoulder. "Got it!"

"We'll tell the others of your sacrifice!" shouted Bridger, almost to the tunnel.

Justin's voice echoed as they dodged inside the tunnel mouth. "GUYYYYYYYYYS!"

42

They ran and ran, the hot exhalations of the tunnel drying their clothes on their bodies. As they ran, the red glow grew stronger and stronger, until it was as bright as day. Finally, panting, they stopped before a gigantic wrought iron gate that barred their path. Joe looked quizzically at Bridger. "What do you reckon?"

"Try it," Bridger suggested. Joe pushed the gate gently, and it swung open onto a nightmare landscape. Opening out into a broad subterranean valley, the terrain was harsh and rocky, with one narrow track winding into the distance. Steam erupted from vents in the ground, while flames danced upon the naked rocks, flourishing, yet consuming nothing. There were no plants, no animals, no water, no wind. Apart from the rumble of a distant volcano, the whole valley was completely silent. Over it all shone the red, sourceless glow, like an unseen sun.

Joe knelt on the ashy path. "She came this way. Look." Sure enough, there were the tracks of Laura's dock shoes, leading away down the trail. "Come on, Bridger." They trudged off into the desolate landscape, following the tracks. There was no turning back now.

The path led over embers and cinders, across deep crevasses bridged by thin stone ribs and through fields where the very ground seemed charred. They walked and walked, for what seemed like days. At last, turning a corner, they came to the end of the path. Joe and Bridger stood stock-still, shocked at the sight before them.

It was an ornate mansion, in elegant Victorian style, with graceful carvings and elaborate curlicues adorning the façade. Broken statuary littered the bed of coals that took the place of a lawn, while lava burbled quietly from a fountain near the entryway. The whole edifice was red, from foundation to pediment.

"Nice digs," said Bridger. "Let's see if anyone's home." He led the way up the red marble steps to the main door. The knob turned easily, and the boys entered cautiously, looking all around in wonder. The mansion's interior was as splendid as the exterior, with frescoes on the ceilings and antique furniture in every room. Creeping down the plush carpeted hallway, Joe suddenly stopped, motioning to Bridger to do the same. With his fingertips, he pushed open the door to a drawing room, revealing a single dark figure hunched over an inlaid escritoire.

This figure was familiar to Joe. He recognized the slick black hair, curling slightly at the nape of the neck, the long white hands with the manicured nails, and the patrician profile as the figure bent over the desk. Most of all, he remembered the cloven hooves tucked under the table, fine for most purposes, but useless for hacky sack. As the door creaked fully open, the figure raised its head. "Hello, devil," said Joe.

"Oh, Jesus," said the devil, then clapped a hand to his mouth. "Pardon my French. It's been a rough couple of days." He gestured them into the room. "Please, sit down. Welcome to Hell." He began to clear papers from his desk, vanishing them with a whoosh of flame. Out of thin air he whisked a blank form, a quill pen, and an ink pot, which he set in the center of his blotter. "I would offer you refreshments, but my staff is, erm, engaged elsewhere. Now, then," he said briskly,

45

inking his pen, "we don't usually get walk-ins, but let's see what we can do for you. Name?"

"Joe Koontz," said Joe. "I've come about my wife."

The devil froze. "Not…Joe Koontz of Missoula?"

"That's right."

The devil buried his head in his hands. "Christ on a stick, this is all I needed. First that banjo-plonking ginger turns all of Hell upside down, and now Joe Koontz, the Hacky Sack Hick Czar of Missoula, shows up to make everything worse. What the hell next?"

"I came, too," said Bridger, peeking over Joe's shoulder. The devil groaned in agony.

Joe hauled a silk-upholstered chair next to the desk and sat, poking the devil's shoulder. "You said my wife was here. Where is she? What have you done with her?"

The devil looked up into Joe's face. "Who, now?"

"My wife, Laura. The banjo-plonking ginger. Purple-streaked hair, tells bad jokes, licks people when they're not looking?"

"*That's* your wife?" The devil let out a dry, humorless laugh. "Figures. You guys deserve each other."

"What happened? What have you done to her?"

The devil exploded. "What have *I* done?! More like, what has *she* done to *me*? Everything was perfect before she came. Everything was just dandy. If only I'd known how it would all change–"

Bridger smacked the devil on the back of the head. "Quit freaking out and tell the story."

The devil drew a deep, shuddering breath. "All right. It was about two days ago, in the evening. I'd gone out past the gate to check on the monster…"

"Yeah, what's with the monster, anyway?" Bridger interrupted. "You have so many people trying to break in here you need a guard lizard?"

The devil shrugged. "It's a style thing. People expect a guardian at the gates of Hell, whether it's Cerberus in Greece or the Flathead Lake Monster in Montana. Kind of adds to the wow factor for the new arrivals."

"Oh, OK," said Bridger. "Carry on."

"Anyway," continued the devil, "I was standing there in the dark, when, echoing down through the water, I could hear the most delightful music. Banjo music." He closed his eyes, enraptured by the memory. "As you know, the banjo is one of my favorite instruments, second only to the accordion. Well, of course I got the monster to take me to the surface for a better listen. And there she was, plonking out "Buffalo Gals," slow and off-key. I knew I had to have her. So the next day, I sent the monster to bring her in."

Joe saw red, though it took him a minute to notice because everything around him was also red. "If you've laid a hand on her…"

The devil looked at Joe blankly, then understood. "What? Oh, oh no, I had no designs on Laura herself. I only wanted

48

to offer her a job." He looked wistfully out the window, over the blazing hellscape. "Gingers, as you know, have no souls, which makes them naturals for employment in Hell. I was going to start her in the third circle, playing for the gluttons, but with hard work, who knows how low she could have descended? It all fell apart so fast."

Joe goggled. "My wife works in Hell?"

"*Worked* in Hell. She only lasted one day." The devil rubbed his temples. "Tell me, did you see anyone on your way in here? Any demons, imps, or lesser devils? Any at all?" Joe shook his head. "Of course you didn't." The devil blew out his cheeks. "That's because they're all on strike."

"Demons can do that?" Joe was incredulous. "Go on strike, I mean? I didn't know they were organized."

"They weren't, until *she* came. She worked half a day, and then all of a sudden, she's sending messages out of the pit saying that she's appalled by the working conditions, that the demons deserve paid vacations and medical coverage and I don't know what all else. And then everything stopped. No torments, no tortures, *nothing* is getting done." The devil paused, his lower lip trembling. "They're demanding tea breaks. TEA BREAKS!" He slammed his fist on the table, breathing hard.

"Get it together, devil," said Joe. "Where is Laura now?"

"I expect she's down at her house, at the edge of the lake of fire. A whole house I gave her, all to herself. Excellent location, convenient to shopping and the cultural district, and this is how she repays me. She's turned it into her headquarters." Turning to Joe, the devil grabbed both his hands. "Couldn't you go and talk to her? Convince her to leave peacefully? I'll be honest, we're in a "Ransom of Red Chief" situation here. I could probably see my way to that Super Rex Racer you didn't get all those years ago." A fancy remote control car whirred out from the corner and parked at Joe's feet. The devil gazed pleadingly into Joe's face. "Be a pal? Please?"

Joe stood, carefully extricating himself from the devil's grip. "I'll talk to her. No promises, though; you know how she is when she's riled. Bridger, stay here with the devil; I'll be back soon." Bridger gave a thumbs-up from deep inside the liquor cabinet, where he was extracting a bottle of Hot Damn and a couple of shot glasses. Joe made his way out the front door and back down the path, backtracking toward the lake of fire.

He heard them before he could see them, the gibbering chants of the demonic rabble floating on the superheated air. As he approached the bungalow on the banks of the lake, they became clear; thousands of small, black, pointy-eared imps, all limbs and claws and teeth. Several jabbed their pitchforks in the air, flapping the tiny signs taped to their tines. As Joe drew closer, he could make out words rising out of the chaotic gabble. "*Un-ion! Un-ion!*" The plonk of a banjo melody threaded through the chant; Joe identified the tune as "Take This Job and Shove It." The notes trailed off as he approached, and a gangly figure appeared, silhouetted in the doorway.

"Better not cross that picket line without me, baby," it said. "Hang on, I'll come get you." Stepping off the porch, Laura waded through the line of imps and gave Joe a big kiss. "Glad you made it. Come on inside."

She led Joe through the picket line and up the steps into a small but comfortable living room. Matilda the banjo reclined in a stand beside an overstuffed sofa. "Make yourself comfortable, honey; I'll make us some tea." Laura headed for the kitchen.

Joe grabbed her hand. "Huckleberry, I've come to take you home. Bridger is distracting the devil; if we leave now, we can make it."

"What? No, I can't leave now!" Laura pulled her hand away. "Look, I promised the imps I'd see this thing through— I'm their leader now. You saw the Man up there in the big house, didn't you? We're sticking it to him; he's just about to cave. We can't quit now!" She turned back towards the kitchen. "Anyway, I kind of like it here. It's always warm and you can't beat the view. We should stay a while." Outside the kitchen window, waves of magma lapped the lake shore.

Joe pouted. "But I miss you. I dove to the bottom of Flathead Lake for you, I fed Justin to the monster for you—"

Laura giggled. "The monster ate Justin?"

"Yep. And then Bridger and I walked all the way across Hell and we went to the devil's house and it's way too hot for all of this, and I really just need you to come home with me."

Laura wavered. "Oh, honey, I do want to come home. Tell you what, if I can just get some of our demands met, then I can leave with a clear conscience." On a scrap of paper, she scribbled a list. "Two weeks of vacation per year, full medical and dental, and two twenty-minute tea breaks per shift should do it." She handed the paper to Joe. "Tell the Man that if he'll agree to those terms, I'll agree to go quietly." She kissed Joe on the forehead. "Be persuasive. I'm counting on you."

So it was that Joe found himself walking back across Hell on yet another of his wife's insane missions. He trotted up the steps of the devil's mansion and opened the door. "Bridger?" he called, entering the hallway. "Devil? You guys here?"

"In here," called Bridger, from the drawing room. Pushing the door open, Joe beheld a scene of chaos. The draperies were torn from their hangings and strewn across the floor. The glass front of the liquor cabinet was shattered, and empty bottles of Hot Damn lay all about the room. Behind an overturned sofa near the wall, a pair of cloven hooves stuck straight up in the air. A gurgling hiccup came from somewhere below them.

"We had a shot for shot contest," Bridger explained, downing another gulp of Hot Damn. "You'd think the devil would hold his liquor better." He tossed the empty bottle over his shoulder with a crash, and resumed playing with the Super Rex toy car, sending it through an intricate series of loops and pivots.

Joe tipped the sofa back on its feet and sat the devil more or less upright on it. He unrolled the paper Laura had given him. "OK, devil, I think I've got a way to solve both of our problems. All you need to do is sign this paper, and she'll agree to leave with me."

The devil looked blearily at Joe, yellow eyes unfocused. "Wha'm I signing?" He took the paper and peered at it. "Looks like a contrack. I like contracks."

"Yes, it's a contract. It says that you'll do these things for the demons, and then Laura will give you what you want."

The devil chuckled. "Wha' I want? She doesn't have anything I want. Doesn't even have a soul." He turned melancholy, dropping his head in self-pity. "I neverrr had a soul…"

Joe shook the devil, and his head popped up. "Joe! How you doin', buddy? Long time no see!" The devil hiccupped again.

Joe gritted his teeth. He grabbed the quill from the escritoire, miraculously still upright, then crouched next to the precariously tilting devil on the sofa, spreading the contract across his knee. "Look, just sign this, would you? It decrees that Friday is henceforth and forevermore Pizza Day in Hell."

"Pizza? I love pizza," said the devil, brightening. He took the quill and signed with a flourish. "Love Pizza Day. Love Pizza Day."

"I'll drink to that," said Joe, retrieving a half-full bottle of Hot Damn from under the liquor cabinet. "Here, after you." One swig later, the devil was snoring on the sofa, and Joe and Bridger were out the door and headed for the lake of fire.

Halfway there, however, Joe stopped. "Hang on," he said to Bridger. "If I know Laura, even with all the demons' demands met, she'll be reluctant to leave." He looked around the burning landscape. "The devil was right, she's a natural for Hell. We'll need something more to tempt her out. Lend me the Super Rex." Taking the control from Bridger, Joe carefully sent the toy car into one of the rivulets of fire that flowed by the path. With several slow, careful corralling maneuvers, he herded something to the edge, then, quick as a flash, ducked down and grabbed, pocketing it before Bridger could see what he had.

Back at Laura's bungalow, Joe waved the contract aloft as he approached the picket line. "Concessions! Concessions from the Man!" he cried. The imps parted, allowing him to pass.

Laura appeared in the doorway. "You did it? You really did it?"

Joe grinned. "You bet. And I got you a gift, too." He dipped his hand into his pocket and came up displaying a tiny, incandescent orb. It pulsed violet in the palm of his hand, its surface glittering like diamonds.

Laura clasped her hands. "For me?"

"For you, Huckleberry. Your very own soul."

"It's beautiful." Laura held out her hand, and the soul jumped into her palm, sparkling happily. "I even like the color."

"I knew you would. Ready to go?"

"Sure thing, honey." Laura tucked the soul in her pocket, slung Matilda across her back, and together our three heroes set out across Hell for the last time. They passed the volcano, they crossed the Gorge of Suffering, and then, at long last, they were past the gates and out of danger.

Well, almost out of danger. At the far end of the tunnel, almost inside the cave, they realized that the Flathead Lake Monster was still at home. And he was awake.

Peering around the corner, Joe, Laura, and Bridger could make out the bulk of the monster moving about in the gloom.

It shuffled around a large, flat stone, like a table top, around which were arranged several smaller stones. On each stone was a doll, and in front of each doll was a small cup and saucer.

"Oh my God," said Bridger. "He's having a tea party."

"That one doll on the end is huge," whispered Laura. "And ugly."

"That's no doll," replied Joe. "That's Justin."

Sure enough, as the monster made the rounds of the table, carefully pouring lake water into each cup from a chipped china teapot, Justin was clearly visible in the place of honor, wearing a too-small pink ruffled frock, a dirty, blonde-ringleted wig, and a fixed, terrified smile. The monster cooed and patted Justin on the head with a single enormous claw, then passed him a plate of imaginary cookies. Justin took one and mimed eating, the grimace of fear never leaving his face.

"The monster will see us for sure if we go for the pool. We'll have to distract it somehow," said Joe. "And we should probably rescue Justin, too."

"Do we have to?" asked Bridger. "And also, how?"

"Stand back," said Laura. "And cover your ears. It's Laura time." She whipped Matilda up in front of her, strummed a few chords, and began to sing (her singing, children, is a little worse than her playing, if you can imagine that). She sang:

Oh, the devil went down to Flathead,

He was looking to fill a position.

He had had no luck, cause his applicants sucked,

So that devil was on a mission.

The monster whined and clutched its ear holes. Tears sprang to Justin's eyes, but he didn't move. Laura continued:

Well, he came across this ginger with a banjo, playing it cool,

He said, come on honey, want to come make some money,

But that devil, he'd end up the fool.

The monster let out an ear-piercing squeal and bounded off down another tunnel, yelping. Justin scrambled down from his stone and ran towards them, tearing off his wig. "Come on, into the pool," yelled Joe. "Hurry!"

"But I have more verses!" Laura protested. The others were already diving in. "Oh, OK, I'll sing them later." She took a running start and jumped.

Under water, she began to drift upward. Slowly, slowly, but steadily she rose, buoyed by the effervescence of the soul in her pocket. Joe held her hand and rose with her, Bridger held on to Joe, Justin held on to Bridger despite his kicking, and together they all bobbed to the surface of the lake, where Tara waited on the dock with towels and a thermos of hot tea.

After tea, Joe and Laura made their way to their cabin, weary and ready for a well-deserved rest. Laura slung her arms comfortably around Joe. "That was quite an adventure, honey, but I'm glad we're back."

Joe hugged her. "Me too."

Laura grinned, then widened her eyes. "Oh, I almost forgot! I have one thing to do before bed!" She felt in her pocket for the soul, pulling it out and examining it. "Whew, still good. Not bruised at all." She crossed the kitchen to the fridge, opened it, and pulled out a bottle of ketchup. Squirting a puddle onto a plate, she dunked the soul into it and took a big bite. "Mmmmm...fresh," she murmured around the mouthful.

"As good as you hoped?" said Joe.

"Mmf," agreed Laura, licking soul juice off her fingers. "Fresh picked is always the best." She winked at Joe, crinkling the new freckle that appeared at the corner of her eye. Gingers, as you know, gain a new freckle whenever they eat a soul. She burped daintily. "Ready for sleep?"

"Been ready," Joe slipped an arm around her waist, and together they went off to catch some Z's, at least until the next adventure.

THE END

How Grandpa Dave Conquered France

Up to now, children, you've heard all about the wild adventures and heroic deeds of your Uncle Joey: how he cheated the devil (twice), vanquished a dragon, and stole the secret of fire from the gods. But did you know, children, that Joe's father, your Grandpa Dave, was just as intrepid, and had just as many brave exploits as Uncle Joey? No? Gather round, then, and hear the story of how Grandpa Dave became the King of France.

It all began, children in the long, long ago, when Dave and his best friend Bill were younger, and they entered the doubles cheese-eating contest at the Missoula County Fair together. The competition was fierce, and in the end it came down to Dave, Bill, a single block of cheddar, and their mad desire to win it all. As the final buzzer sounded, Dave stuffed the last bite of cheese into his face, raised his arms in victory, and then collapsed onto the stage next to Bill like an elephant seal having a stroke. The audience thundered its applause as Bill and Dave were helped into the bed of a waiting pickup truck and trundled off home to recover.

The next day, Dave was lying on his couch, trying to sleep off his horrendous cheese hangover, when he heard a rap on the door. "Could you get that?" he said to Bill, who was sprawled on the other couch across the room.

Bill paddled his arms and legs in the air, trying to regain verticality, but to no avail. "Doesn't look like it," he said.

"OK, hang on. I have an idea." After some deft maneuvering with a pool cue that had been fortuitously lying nearby, Dave managed to open the door without getting up, revealing two elegant men wearing tailcoats and blue silk sashes across their chests. Dave waved them inside, then poked the door closed with the cue.

"Mr. Koontz? I'm John Wallace, the organizer of the cheese-eating contest at the county fair. You and Mr. Farrell left last night without claiming your trophy, so I've taken the liberty of bringing it to you."

"Hey, cool." Dave extended the cue towards Wallace, hooking the trophy by the handle and passing it over to Bill. "We're champions."

"Erm, yes," said Wallace. "Congratulations. And may I present Monsieur Gerard, the chairman of the French League of Cheesemakers." The other man, tall and thin with an impeccably waxed mustache, made a courtly bow. Dave waved the cue in welcome. "Howdy."

"*Bonjour*, Monsieur Koontz. And may I say, I hope that you will very much enjoy your sojourn in my country."

"Huh?" Dave rolled sideways off the couch, landing on all fours, and got to his feet with a herculean heave.

Gerard produced a blue ticket envelope from his inside his coat. "*Oui*, Monsieur Koontz. I am pleased to be your escort on your voyage to France, which you have won through your efforts last night."

"OK, back up," said Bill, from the sofa. "We're going to France? What the hell for?"

"It's a collaboration between the Montana Dairy Farmer's Association and the League of Cheesemakers," explained Wallace.

"We call it *Fromage* Across the Ocean," said Gerard.

"Indeed. We're seeking to inspire the next generation of cheese producers through a series of grants for travel to the world's cheesiest regions. And since you've proved your dedication to the concept of cheese last night, Monsieur Gerard and I can think of nobody more worthy of a free trip to France for a comprehensive cheese-sampling tour." Wallace dabbed away the sweat that had sprung from his forehead at the mere thought of so much cheese. "You leave tomorrow morning."

Dave turned to Bill. "Any plans tomorrow?"

"None that I can think of."

Dave turned back to Wallace and Gerard. "All right, then. See you tomorrow at the airport."

Gerard bowed again, Wallace shook Dave and Bill's hands, and in a twinkling, the two were gone. Dave shuffled into the bedroom, and in a moment there came the sound of a zipper unzipping, followed by thumps and rustling. Bill tilted off the sofa, righted himself with an effort, and rolled after Dave. "Whatcha doing in here?"

"Packing. You think I should take the .270, or the .308?" Dave held up a pair of deer rifles for Bill's appraisal.

"Take 'em both. Better to have 'em and not need 'em." (This was a time, children, when baggage on plane rides was free, and you could take as many guns as you wanted. Everything is worse now.)

"Good thinking." Dave tossed the rifles into the duffel bag on the bed. "Two handguns be enough, you think?"

"Better make it three. Don't forget the ammo." Dave nodded agreement, and added the pistols, plus a couple pairs of underoos. He zipped up the bulging duffel. "There. Now we're traveling Montana-style!"

Fast forward two weeks. After a long plane ride, Dave and Bill had reunited with Monsieur Gerard, who had immediately commenced hauling them all over France, from

Normandy to Nice, tasting cheese after cheese after cheese. A sample of entries from Dave's diary reveals their growing discontent:

Day 6: Tour of Le Musée de Fromage et Fraternité. Haven't pooped since Montana. And

Day 347: More fucking cheese.

Finally, they arrived at the grand finale of their tour: Paris! Monsieur Gerard, a native Parisian, was in top form as he led them through the first of their stops for the day, the Cluny Monastery on the banks of the Seine. He waved his hands as they wended through the medieval passageways. "The brothers of Cluny, monsieurs, were famous for two things: their champagne, and their cheese. And *oui*, there are some tapestries around here somewhere, but nobody much cares about them." He pushed open a heavy oaken door, revealing a room full of steel vats, tanks, and piping. "*Regardez-vous*: the champagnery. The formula has been unchanged for centuries, though now the monks use a modern pressurized carbonation system." He let the door swing shut on a disappointed Dave and Bill. "Onward, monsieurs, to the cheesery!" Bill sighed,

Dave groaned, but out of politeness they trudged after the prattling Gerard.

Suddenly from the courtyard outside, came the most ungodly howling Dave and Bill had ever heard, followed by shrieks of terror. *"La Bête!"* a voice screamed. *"La Bête de Gevaudan!"* The scream cut off abruptly, replaced by a low grumbling growl and the sound of something feeding.

The Beast of Gevaudan, as you know, children, was a creature that terrorized the French countryside in the 18th century, devouring men, women and children as they herded livestock in the forest. Though historically thought to have been a hyena escaped from the royal menagerie, the Beast has been called everything from a werewolf to a demon from Hell. It ceased its attacks in 1767, perhaps killed in one of many extermination hunts organized by the King.

What you most likely do not know, children, for the French do not like to talk about it, is that a mad Parisian scientist-turned-monk, inspired by the real-life story, set out to create a latter-day Beast of Gevaudan using surgery, radiation, and genetic manipulation. Though nobody knew for certain what he had done, rumors flew that the animal he had created was far larger, far toothier, and much, much more aggressive than its predecessor. And on this day, when Dave and Bill just happened to be in Paris, it had killed its maker and escaped containment. And it was hungry.

Frozen in place, they heard the sound of a distant door being nosed open, followed by the click of claws on flagstones. "It is inside," whispered the white-faced Gerard. "Hasten, monsieurs, to the dungeon, and lock yourselves in. I will go to warn the brothers." He hustled off down the passage.

Dave tugged at Bill's sleeve. "Come on, follow me."

"No, not that way. The dungeon is down this hallway, remember?"

"We're not going to the dungeon." Dave led the way through the maze of medieval masonry, ears pricked for the sounds of the beast. "Here we are. Gatehouse." He shoved aside the partially devoured remains of the gatekeeper and reached under the counter, pulling out his trusty duffel bag from where he had stowed it on the way in. "I was mad when the hotel wouldn't let us stash our bags there until check-in, but now it looks like it was good luck." He unzipped the bag and began to unpack, tossing one of the rifles to Bill. "Here's what we're going to do…"

A few minutes later, Bill crept towards the great hall of the monastery, following the slavering, panting noises of the feeding beast. Through the cracked door he could see it shaking back and forth, tearing flesh, then tossing its head to gulp the meat down. Hooked on one fang was a scrap of blue silk that Bill recognized as a piece of Gerard's sash. It was too late for him, but if Bill acted quickly, he could save the rest of Paris.

He kicked the door open. "Hey, Beast! Fuck you!" He opened fire with the pistols, emptying both magazines. Bullets thudded into the beast's black fur; blood spurted onto the stone floor. The monster reared onto its hind legs and howled. Bill shouldered the rifle and fired two shots at the center of the beast's chest. Roaring in pain and fury, it dropped to all fours and charged.

Bill turned and fled down the passage, trying not to think about the yellow eyes behind him, the thump of paws steadily gaining ground. He zigged and zagged, using the monster's bulk against it. Grabbing the doorjamb of the champagnery, he swung himself inside, the beast's teeth clicking on empty space as it snapped and missed. It shouldered into the room as Bill turned and backed away, placing his feet carefully on the steel catwalk over the champagne vats. "Come on, you ugly son of a bitch. That's it." he taunted. "Come and get me."

"Bill, get down!" shouted Dave from the shadows. Bill dropped to his belly as Dave fired his .308. There was a loud *ping* as the bullet ricocheted. *God, don't tell me he missed*, thought Bill.

But no, there came a deafening whoosh as Dave's bullet punctured one of the CO_2 carbonation canisters arrayed against the wall. It took off like a rocket, rattling to and fro amongst the piping, then, with a clang, it bounced off the side of a fermentation tank and barreled into the beast's side, knocking it off the catwalk and into the vat. Its snarls became wails of terror as it scrabbled its claws against the curved steel, unable to find purchase. Finally, struggling and gurgling, it sank, floating down through the clear champagne to rest on the bottom.

Dave joined Bill on the catwalk, and together they stared down through the champagne at the enormous dead beast. "Well," said Dave. "Shit. I guess we should go back to the hotel and figure out who we need to tell about this."

"Sounds good to me," replied Bill. "Let's reload on the way out in case there are more critters." They slung their rifles over their shoulders, stuck the pistols in their belts, and, collecting their bags at the gatehouse, set off down the road.

"This is really weird," observed Dave, looking right and left as they walked down the Champs Eliseés.

"Where is everyone?" asked Bill. For the streets were completely still and silent. Cars, abandoned, sat in the boulevards with their doors open and seats empty. The barest breath of wind stirred the leaves in the trees. From time to time, Dave would catch a flicker of motion at the periphery of his vision, but before he could turn to look, it vanished.

Dave shrugged. "No idea. And to top it all off, I'm pretty sure we're lost." They had been wandering the streets of Paris for hours by now, and had completely lost their bearings. Dave pointed at an enormous building with an ornate marble façade. "There's got to be someone in there who can help us find our way back to the hotel. Let's go in there and ask." Re-settling their rifles across their shoulders, they climbed the broad steps up to the colonnade.

Their footsteps echoed on the marble floor. Bill peeked down a long, frescoed gallery. "Nobody here, either."

Dave was growing frustrated. "This whole damn country is crazy." He pulled one of the pistols from his belt and racked the slide. "Here, I'll just fire a signal shot. See if anybody–"

"WE SURRENDER!" a voice screamed from the shadows. A gray-haired man wearing an immaculate suit dived out from behind a column and flung himself prone at Dave's feet. "Please, monsieur," he begged, clutching at Dave's sneakers. "We give up, the day is yours. Please do not shoot."

"Monsieur le President is sincere," echoed another voice. "We will not resist. Please do not harm us." Dave peered around the column to see another elderly man, this one wearing an elaborate chain of office, also prostrate on the marble.

Dave sighed. He leaned down and grabbed the collar of the President of France, trying to heave him up, but the man was dead weight. "Come on, Pierre, pull it together. Nobody's getting shot today. Well, nobody else," he said, remembering the dead beast back at the monastery.

The president looked up, tears streaming down his bulldog cheeks. "You accept our surrender?"

Dave sighed again. "Fine. Whatever. Sure."

The president's face suddenly was wreathed in smiles. "Then we are saved! Monsieur le Mayor, get up, tell the people to come out, the danger is past!" He ran to the top of the steps. "*Mes amis!* You can come out now, the strangers have accepted our surrender!" There was movement in the streets. From market stalls, from under benches, out from flower beds, like the Munchkins at the beginning of *The Wizard of Oz*, crept the French. They began to mass at the foot of the steps. The president waved his arms. "My brothers, our long national nightmare is over. At long last, we have a new king! His name is—" The president swung back to whisper to Dave. "Your name again, Majesty?"

"Um, Dave. This is my friend Bill."

"*Oui*, and you are from where?"

"Missoula."

"*Trés bien.*" The president faced the crowd again, arms upflung. "King Dave the First! And his dear friend Guillaume, le Comte de Missoula!"

The crowd erupted. "*Vive le roi! Vive le comte! Vive le roi!*"

Bill leaned over to Dave. "What now?"

"God, I don't know. Just go with it, I guess." Before he could say more, the crowd had whisked Dave and Bill onto its shoulders and carried them off towards the palace.

Fast-forward again, just one day. Dave stood in an ornate bedroom, adjusting his crown in a full-length gilded mirror, which was difficult because the sleeves of his ermine robes kept getting in his way. Bill reclined on a velvet sofa, a box of bon-bons balanced on his belly. The Lord Chamberlain, a round, bespectacled man, stood nervously behind Dave with a clipboard. "Majesty, a few points regarding the festivities you have ordered in honor of your coronation…"

"Shoot, Pierre."

The Lord Chamberlain, whose name was Etienne, winced. "Firstly, how do you say, the turkey shoot. I regret to say, Majesty, that the turkey, he is not native to France."

"Lame. What *do* you have in France?"

"Pheasants, Majesty."

"Nail some fans to their butts. Nobody will know the difference." From the sofa, Bill chuckled around a bon-bon. "Next problem?"

"The hunting robes that you have ordered, Majesty…I regret that the ermine traditionally used does not come in this "blaze orange" you specify."

Dave pointed at the Lord Chamberlain in the mirror. "Spray paint."

The Lord Chamberlain sighed. "Yes, Majesty."

"Any other problems I can help you with, Pierre?"

"Not at the moment, Majesty."

"Then we'd best get a move on before we miss the banquet. Come on, Bill." Dave swept out of the room and down the grand staircase towards the great hall, Bill in his wake, leaving a trail of half-eaten bon-bons.

As Dave entered, shouts of *"Vive le roi!"* echoed through the hall, as all the people bowed deeply. He regally waved them to their seats, taking his place at the head of the table. "Let the banquet begin!" White-gloved waiters leaned forward and whisked off silver covers, revealing steaming dishes underneath.

Dave poked tentatively with his fork. "What the hell is this?" he asked the Mayor of Paris, who was seated to his left.

"Frogs' legs, Majesty."

"Uh-huh. And these?"

"*Escargot*, Majesty. The snails."

Bill picked one up between thumb and forefinger. "What am I supposed to do with this?"

"Open it, Monsieur le Comte, with the tongs. Regard." The mayor deftly cracked a snail and slurped it down, leaving a smear of mucus in his beard.

Dave blanched. "You know, we're not real hungry. Maybe we should just have dessert and call it a night."

"Of course, Majesty." The mayor clapped his hands, and a waiter appeared, bearing a silver covered platter adorned with intricate scrollwork and filigree. In a single motion, he whipped away the cover, revealing its contents.

Bill screamed. Dave looked as though he might faint. For there in the center of the platter, surrounded by fresh strawberries, lay an enormous, obscene wedge of Brie cheese.

Dave made his decision. "You know," he said slowly. "I've had just about enough." Deliberately, he took off his crown and laid it on the table. "I never thought I'd say this, but there's such a thing as too much cheese. Come on, Bill." He shrugged out of his robes, and amid the stunned silence of the French, he and Bill made their way out of the hall and out of the palace. Outside, they stole the Lord Chamberlain's Peugeot and drove it to the airport, where they caught the soonest flight back to Missoula. And thus ended the one-day reign of King Dave the First.

So, children, if we are going to be strictly technical, your grandfather was a king, which makes you both Princesses of France, entitled to all the privileges thereof. Remind your mother of that the next time she won't let you have any ice cream. She will be very impressed.

THE END

Lauren and the Bearsnake

Once upon a time, there was a little girl named Lauren, who lived in Montana with her mother, her father, and her big sister Renee. In the spring, they took their dog Murphy for walks among the wildflowers; in the fall, they played in piles of fallen leaves; and in the winter they built snow forts and slid on the ice. But Lauren's favorite season was summer, because that was when her family took their camper to a campground beside a lake, where they played and swam and ran through the woods with lots of other children. The fun lasted from morning to night, and Lauren's very favorite part was the evenings, when she and her sister would dance in the dark with glow sticks and make s'mores around the campfire.

It was on just such a summer evening that Lauren went into the woods with her sister and friends for one last game of hide and seek before the sun set completely. The pine needles were whispering in the breeze, the last sunlight was shimmering on the lake, and the T-rexes were beginning their frolics by the shore, as they often do in Montana. It was Lauren's turn to hide, and as Renee leaned against a tree, counting to a hundred, she slipped off into the brush, looking for just the perfect spot.

She slid down hills and crawled under logs, but didn't find any places that would be just right for hiding. The light grew dimmer and dimmer as she went farther, until suddenly Lauren realized that she couldn't hear the other children anymore. The wind picked up a bit, and it was getting cold, so she decided that it might be a good idea to go back to camp, tag out of hide and seek, and go see if anyone was making dinner. She turned and began to walk back in the direction she had come.

Suddenly, she sensed that she was not alone. At first it was just a feeling, a prickling of the short hairs on the back of her neck. And then she heard the sound.

Grrrrrsssssssss. Grrrrrrrsssssssss. It was coming from behind her. Lauren froze. "It's probably just the wind," she whispered to herself, though she knew that the wind didn't growl like that.

Grrrrrrrrsssss. Grrrrrrssss. It was getting louder. It was getting closer. Lauren knew she had to look. Slowly, trembling, she turned.

There was nothing in the shadows behind her. No, wait, there was something there, coiled and shifting in the darkness between two trees. Lauren could make out tufts of shaggy fur, and the rising moon glinted off what looked like scales. She stared, fascinated, as the creature rose and stretched upwards. It turned its head towards her, and the moonlight caught its eyes, glowing red like coals. It growl-hissed again, and that was enough for Lauren. She turned and fled, shrieking, through the woods.

She ran and ran, screaming her head off until she thought her lungs would burst. She could see the glow of campfires ahead. Pelting along at top speed, she was going too fast to stop when a tall, gangly shape stepped out from the trees in front of her. Like a strand of pasta thrown against a wall, Lauren ran splat into her Uncle Joe.

"What's going on, Squirt?" Joe asked, picking her up off the ground and swinging her up piggyback-style. "The whole campground could hear you yelling. Are you hurt?"

"I heard a sound!" Lauren sobbed, clinging to Joe's neck.

"What kind of sound? Also, don't strangle the horsie," gurgled Joe, loosening her death grip on his throat as they walked.

"A really scary sound! It was either a bear or a snake!" Lauren was calming down a little, but she still shook and whimpered. "I want my mommy!"

Joe chuckled quietly. "You heard a bearsnake, huh? I hear they get bold this time of year. Come right into the campsite, they will." They were almost back at Lauren's family's camper. She jumped off Joe's back and ran the rest of the way to the camper door, where her mom was unpacking marshmallows for s'mores.

"Mommy, open the door! There's a bearsnake after me!" Lauren dived inside the camper and ran to her bed, burrowing underneath the blankets and pillows. Her mother sighed and followed, flipping on the lights and pulling the top pillow off to reveal the terrified little girl beneath. "All right, what has your Uncle Joey been telling you now?"

"Hey, I'm innocent!" said Joe, holding up his hands. "She came running out of the woods screaming that she heard something that was either a bear or a snake. Clearly, it was a bearsnake."

Lauren's mom sighed even bigger. "Lauren, honey, Uncle Joe was just teasing you. There's no such thing as a bearsnake."

"Says *you*," said Joe from the fridge, where he was rummaging for cookies.

"You probably just heard a chipmunk in the leaves. Come on out of there, now, and we'll go make s'mores. Grandpa is just getting the fire going now."

"Nuh-uh." Lauren grabbed the pillow and plopped it back on top of her nest, sealing herself in. "There *is* a bearsnake. I heard it. And I saw it."

"Fine. Whatever. Stay inside if you want, but you're going to miss a lot of fun." Lauren's mom turned and left, pausing

84

on her way out to smack Joe on the back of the head. Lauren huddled down into as tight a ball as she could. From outside the camper, she could see the glow of the fire and hear the low murmur of conversation, punctuated by squeals from the other children as they played among the trees. Finally, very late, she fell asleep.

The next morning, Lauren was the last to wake up. She wandered outside, bed-headed, to the table where everyone was having a pancake picnic.

"What's up, Squirt? We missed you last night. Don't worry, though, I ate your s'more for you, so it wasn't wasted." Uncle Joe was dousing a stack of huckleberry pancakes in syrup.

"We played with glow sticks and danced to music with those kids from the tent by the lake," said Lauren's sister Renee. "Aunt Laura says it's called a rave. It was really fun."

Lauren moped. She could have had a s'more and gone to the rave, if it hadn't been for the dumb bearsnake. But what if it came back again tonight? Or all the other nights at camp?

She couldn't hide in the camper forever. She decided that she had to do something about the bearsnake.

After breakfast, she went around the camp, gathering supplies. On the back porch of a cabin, she found an old milk crate; from the firewood pile, she got a length of twine. A search of the woods yielded a long, sturdy stick, and at lunch, she pocketed a handful of jelly beans from an unguarded candy bowl. By twilight, she was ready. She headed off into the woods, towards the spot where she had seen the bearsnake.

There was still plenty of light when she reached the right place, so she had no trouble setting her trap. She tilted the milk crate up on one edge, propping it with the stick so it formed an inviting little cave. To the stick she tied the twine, running it out and tucking the other end behind a large tree. Finally, she baited the trap, pouring out the jelly beans into a pile underneath the crate. She ran to where she had set the free end of the twine, curled up with her back against the trunk, and waited.

The light began to fade, and the shadows lengthened. There was no sound except the chatter of birds and the distant rumbles of the occasional T-rex, stretching its limbs as it awoke for the evening. As the sun went down, even the birds fell silent. Lauren was beginning to lose hope in her plan. And then she heard it.

Sssssssssgrrrrrrr. Sssssssgrrrrrrr. The sound was getting louder. Lauren's heart was in her throat.

Sssssssgrrrr. Sssssssgrrrrrr. Closer. Closer. A snuffling noise. A *thunk*, as something bumped the crate. And then, finally, the munching sound of jelly beans being eaten.

Lauren yanked the string, heard the crate slam down. There was a panicked squeak, followed by a loud *SSSSSSSSGRRRRRRR!* *SSSSSSSSSSSSSGRRRRRRRRR!* Peeking around the tree, she saw the crate rocking back and forth, as whatever was inside thrashed to get out. She needed to get help before it escaped.

She ran towards the campground, shouting at the top of her lungs. "I caught it! I caught the bearsnake! Come and see, I caught the bearsnake!"

Uncle Joe, sitting at a picnic table with a bottle of cider, rose and stretched. "You caught the bearsnake? All right, all right, I'll come see. Lead the way." He killed his cider, and snagged a flashlight that was sitting on the edge of the table.

"C'monnnnnnn, before it gets away." Lauren half-led, half-dragged Joe into the woods.

The crate was still in the same spot, still rocking slightly, though the hiss-growls from inside were a little fainter. Lauren crept up behind Joe as he crouched down to peer inside, playing the flashlight over the crate's occupant.

The creature was hideous. Its head was smooth and scaly and green, with lidless eyes like yellow diamonds, glittering malevolently in the flashlight beam. As the neck sloped toward the shoulders, at some indeterminate border the scales ceased, blending into matted, stinking brown fur. The body was stocky and stubby; there was no tail to speak of, and the legs terminated in broad, clawed, stumpy paws. The animal hiss-growled again, cringing away from the humans. "See," whispered Lauren, "there *is* a bearsnake. I caught it, and this is proof."

"Welllll, not exactly, Squirt," replied Joe. as he played the light over the animal. "I'm afraid what you have here is a snakebear. They're pretty common around here, and they're completely harmless. We should probably let this one go on his way before too long."

"NO! It's the bearsnake, I know it!" Lauren stamped her feet. She had worked hard to catch her bearsnake, and she wasn't about to let Uncle Joe release it again, just when she had conquered it.

"OK, confession time," said Joe, a little sheepishly. "Your mom was right, there's no such thing as a bearsnake. I made it up to tease you." Lauren glared. "No, really, cross my heart. Bearsnakes are made up. I promise." Joe tipped the crate up on its side, and the snakebear scuttled out, hiss-growling all the way to the trees. It rustled and grumbled through the undergrowth for a moment or two, and then it was gone.

Joe bent down. "Come on, Squirt, I'll give you a piggyback back to camp. We can come back for your trap in the morning." Lauren scowled. Silently, deliberately, she gathered her milk crate, her string, and her stick. She pocketed the jellybean bait, and without a glance at Joe, she stamped back towards camp.

It was a long evening. While the other children splashed in the lake shallows, hunting for crayfish, Lauren stayed parked on her bed in the camper with a pad of paper and a box of crayons. Bit by bit, she sketched in the plans for a new, improved bearsnake trap. By bedtime, she had a plan.

She spent the whole next day building her trap. The milk crate and stick idea was solid, she decided, but she needed a backup plan, in case the bearsnake turned out to be more feisty than the snakebear. More than that, she had to bring the bearsnake back to camp, make everyone look at it, and prove that she was right and they were wrong. She'd show them all.

At twilight, she set off once more into the woods. The milk crate and stick contraption now rode on top of a rude sled that she had fashioned out of a stray boogie board from the beach and a pair of runners made from cut-up beer cans and duct tape, along with a coil of strong rope that she had found behind a shed at the camp. When she reached the bearsnake's clearing again, she propped up the crate, tied on her string, and baited the trap with some Skittles (she had accidentally eaten the jelly beans while drawing the night before). Then she took the rope and looped it, making a giant snare that surrounded the crate contraption. Tucking herself behind a large tree, the free end of the string in one hand and the rope in the other, she waited.

At first moonlight, she heard it once again: *Grrrrrsssss. Grrrrrsssss.* There would be no mistake this time. The growl-hiss came closer. Closer. Closer.

Nothing.

The sound had stopped. Lauren frowned. The crate trap stood by itself in a circle of silver moonlight.

Perhaps the bearsnake was cautious, circling the clearing to make sure it was safe. Or perhaps she had spooked it, and it was gone. She stepped forward to peer into the trees, into the light, breaking cover.

Suddenly, there was a loud crash from above, and a huge weight dropped onto Lauren, pinning her to the ground. As she struggled to rise, she could hear the familiar *grrrrrrsssss*, *grrrrrsssssss*. Strong coils wrapped around her limbs as the bearsnake secured its prey. Its hot breath hit her face like a furnace blast as it gaped, preparing to bite.

Lauren tried to scream for help, but could not: the coils were squeezing the breath out of her. With her one free arm, she punched at the bearsnake's furry, short-muzzled head. Its teeth broke the skin of her knuckles, and it growl-hissed in surprise and, for one critical second, it relaxed its grip on Lauren.

It was enough. Lauren lunged and grabbed the thick rope she had used to make her backup snare. One-handed, she flung it, looping it over and around the bearsnake's throat and pulling tight. It snapped at her, sharp teeth clicking inches from her face, and with a second loop of rope, she wrapped its jaws shut, holding on for her life.

She could not have told how long the fight lasted. The coils tightened, and Lauren pulled the rope, until, at some point, the bearsnake began to loosen its grip. Lauren began to breathe a little easier, freeing her other arm from the encircling scales. Through the snare holding its jaws shut, the bearsnake wheezed and whined, now trying to abandon the battle and flee. Lauren gave the rope a final wrench, and the last of the coils fell away. The bearsnake lay in a giant puddle around her feet, still alive, but too weak to fight any further. The first light of shell-pink dawn was just beginning to show through the trees.

It was time for Phase Two. Lauren looped the rope around itself, twisting it behind the bearsnake's head. It was, as you might expect, the opposite of the snakebear, with a furry, round-eared head and a long, scaly, serpentine body. It stirred, beginning to revive, just as Lauren finished tying the last knot in the crude bridle.

Grrrrsss—. The bearsnake's angry growl was cut short as Lauren twitched the bridle hard, jerking its head down. "Knock it off," she warned it sternly. "We have something important to do." The bearsnake subsided, watching her with scowling red eyes.

"That's better." Carefully, Lauren walked around behind the bearsnake, keeping hold of the reins. "All right, then." She took a deep breath, counted, *one, two, three*, and with a sudden leap, vaulted onto the bearsnake's back, a couple of feet behind its head.

It lurched and bucked, trying to shed its burden, but Lauren held on tight. "Settle down, now. We have one more thing to do, and then you can go." She turned its head towards camp. "That way. Giddyup." The bearsnake grumbled, but obeyed, slithering off through the lightening woods.

Uncle Joe, Aunt Laura, and Grandpa Dave were down at the dock, just readying their boat for a morning of fishing, when the girls' mother came running up. "Have any of you seen Lauren?" she gasped. She's not in the camper, and she's not answering when I call her. I've been looking everywhere."

Grandpa Dave straightened up from his tackle box. "OK, we'll help you look. She's a little girl, she can't have gone far. And if she hasn't turned up in half an hour, we'll call the police."

"Found her." Aunt Laura was pointing towards the treeline, where a figure that was undeniably Lauren had just emerged, riding what was indisputably a bearsnake.

"Well, I'll be damned," said Uncle Joey, as Lauren nudged the bearsnake in the ribs, urging it closer to the little group. It slithered towards the dock, growl-hissing under its breath.

Lauren pulled the bearsnake to a stop about ten feet away and cupped her hands around her mouth, hollering to make sure everyone heard. "*I TOLD YOU SO!*" she bellowed.

Uncle Joey raised his hands in acknowledgement. "Sorry I doubted you, Squirt."

Lauren climbed down to the ground. "All right, that was all I needed," she said to the bearsnake. "Hold still." She hooked her fingers around the back of the rope bridle and slid it off the creature's snout. "We're done. Go home." The bearsnake shook its head and snorted. Lauren flicked the reins at its nose. "Go on now, get." It chuffled once more, then dipped its head and slithered off into the trees, disappearing in an instant.

Lauren turned back toward her family, staring them down for a moment. Then, with an audible *harrumph*, she spun and strode back to the camper to wait for breakfast.

Six weeks later. Summer was over, school was about to start again, and Renee, Lauren, and their mother were downtown, shopping for back-to-school supplies.

"Nnnnngh," moaned Lauren, plodding along behind her mother and sister. She would have rather been almost anywhere else.

"Less complaining, please, Lauren," said her mother, consulting a list on a scrap of notebook paper. "We still need shoes for both of you, your sister needs a new lunch box, and you've almost outgrown last year's jacket." She led the way down the sidewalk towards the next shop. Lauren rolled her eyes and followed.

Suddenly the screech of an electronic alarm split the air, followed by screams of "Stop him! Help, police!" A gangly, mangy-looking man pelted around the corner full-tilt, a stuffed satchel in one hand, a snub-nosed revolver in the other. He looked around wildly, gasped, and then plunged down a side street. A few stray dollar bills escaped from his satchel and fluttered in his wake.

A besuited man appeared around the corner, his mouth an O of shock and indignation. "Stop him!" he shouted again. "He just robbed my bank! Someone call the police!"

"Girls, get back to the car," their mother ordered sharply. "This is no place for us. Renee, quickly. Lauren—" she gulped, looking around in bewilderment. "Lauren?"

Blocks away, the bank robber was doubled over, hands on his knees, sucking air. The satchel sat on the ground beside him. He glanced swiftly up and down the road. No sign of pursuit. All he had to do was catch his breath, act naturally, and saunter to his getaway car with the booty. He grinned in his chewed-on beard. He had done it.

"HAAAAAAAEEEEEEEEEE!" The robber barely had time to register the shadow overhead before he was pinned to the ground by a little girl who had leaped off the fire escape above. She was surprisingly strong, wrapping her arms and legs around his, immobilizing him. Her sharp little teeth dug into his shoulder, latching on with an unbreakable viselike grip. He shrieked aloud for mercy as he struggled on the pavement.

Which was how the cops found them, following the sounds of his screams. They promptly arrested him, returned the money to the bank, and pried Lauren's jaws off his shoulder, not necessarily in that order.

"I told you, Mom, I'm fine." Lauren kicked her feet under the plastic seat in the doctor's examination room.

"You are not fine," said her mother sternly. "You jumped off a twelve-foot fire escape and tackled a grown man to the ground. That is not normal. You need to be seen." The sound of well-heeled footsteps came from the hall outside, and the door swung open to reveal the doctor.

"Howdy, folks," he greeted them sunnily. "How're we all doing?"

"Fine," said Lauren.

"Not fine," corrected her mother. "Any results, doctor? Any idea what's wrong with Lauren?"

"Well, I think we have some leads," the doctor began, plopping into a spare chair. He leaned down to Lauren's eye level. "Tell me, Lauren, have you been playing in the woods lately? The deep woods? Like, out by the lake, maybe?"

"We were camping out that way about a month and a half ago," her mother interjected.

"I see. And did you have contact with any wild animals while you were there?"

Lauren nodded hard. "I did. I caught a real bearsnake while I was there. By myself. I did it. It was me."

"I see," the doctor said again. "And did this bearsnake bite you, by any chance? Even the smallest bite?"

"There was a big fight when I captured it," replied Lauren. "I skinned my knuckles on its teeth." She displayed her right hand, the knuckles now healed to smooth pink scars.

The doctor blew out his cheeks. "I see. Well, that would definitely explain the symptoms. Young lady," he said gravely, "I think it's likely that you are a were-bearsnake."

"A *what?*" yelped Lauren's mother.

"A were-bearsnake," repeated the doctor patiently. "As you know, bearsnakes are quite rare in this part of the country, but after some documented contacts, people have reported strange behaviors, such as an inclination to climb, and a desire to spring upon people from great heights, wrestle them to the ground, and bite the living daylights out of them. I have a pamphlet here that might help to explain it." He passed across a folded brochure, with *So, You're a Were-Bearsnake* printed in large type across the top. "I'm afraid it's incurable, though the good news is that it's rarely contagious. Young Lauren here can bite all the people she wants, and the risk of infecting someone else is almost zero.

Lauren's mother unfolded the pamphlet. "This can't be real."

"Oh, it's very real. Here, let me show you some video we took though the microscope when we were examining Lauren's blood sample." The doctor tapped a screen on the wall, selected from a couple of menus, and brought up a new window. "Now, here you can plainly see the normal blood cells, the red, the white, and so on. And here, if we zoom in," he pinched, "you can clearly see the bearsnakes."

Sure enough, in between the corpuscles, there drifted dozens of tiny, squiggly, bear-headed snakes. One snarled at the microscope light as it made its way across the field.

Lauren's mother buried her head in her hands. "She jumped off a twelve-foot fire escape and bit a bank robber into submission."

The doctor grunted. "That would make sense. The bearsnake is an ambush predator." He closed Lauren's chart. "Any questions?" he asked.

"Am I going to turn into a bearsnake?" said Lauren.

"No, I don't think so. Previous cases have almost all involved the acquisition of bearsnake-like abilities. Transmogrification is very rare."

"So, it's more like I have super powers?"

The doctor shrugged. "If you consider climbing and pouncing to be super powers, sure."

"Most excellent." Lauren grinned. This was going to be fun.

THE END

Joe and the Lost City

Time travel, children, is not a real thing. There's no machine that can fly you forward to a future of flying cars and robot servants, no magic spell that will catapult you back to the Renaissance to chat with Leonardo da Vinci. It's just not a thing that can happen. Which, if you think about it, just makes this next story all the more astonishing.

It all began, children, with a hunting trip in the wooded canyons of northern Montana. Your Uncle Joey and Grandpa Dave were trundling up a narrow trail in Dave's trusty, rusty Suburban, eyes peeled for deer sign. The road was narrow and wound up and up, sheer cliff face to the left of the car, a dizzying drop-off on the right. The snow that had fallen all day was thickening, almost blotting out the sunlight. It had been hours since they had seen any tracks. "You know where we are, right?" said Joey, apprehensively.

"Sure I do," replied Dave. "Bill and I used to come up here after mule deer all the time after we got back from France."

Uncle Joey rolled his eyes. He'd heard endless "back when I was the king of France" and "have I ever told you about the time I conquered France" stories throughout his childhood, and it was starting to get old. "OK, Dad," he said. "Long as you can get us home again."

Grandpa Dave peered over the steering wheel. "Probably." Up ahead, jagged rocks poking through the snow marked the end of the road. There was no room for the massive Suburban to turn around. "But it looks like this is the end of the line. Hang on, I'll reverse us out of here."

"Suits me." Uncle Joey had seen his dad drive backwards for miles to get out of sticky situations. He settled back against the seat, letting his baseball cap fall over his eyes. There would be time for a nap, then a Malibu cocktail over lunch once they reached home.

Dozing, Joey did not immediately register the sound of crumbling rock. With a lurch, the back of the Suburban dipped as the edge of the road disintegrated under the right rear tire. "Shit!" shouted Dave, gunning the engine and cranking the wheel hard left, but it was too late. Groaning like a gut-shot brontosaurus, the Suburban lost its footing and slipped over the cliff edge, tumbling end over end towards the valley floor.

The fall seemed to last forever. Trees, rocks, snow, and sky flashed past Joey's view through the shattered windshield. The Suburban rolled and rolled, until it came to rest with a final crunch, upside down against a giant fir. There was stillness. Then, from the driver's side window there slithered a camouflage-clad figure. "Son?" called Dave. "You all right?"

"I think so." Joey was levering himself out of the passenger side, squeezing between the crumpled door and the tree trunk. "You?"

"I'm fine. But we're in one hell of a pickle." Dave regarded the wrecked Suburban. "I don't think old Lucille is going to walk away from this one."

"No kidding." Joe kicked a piece of shredded tire rubber. "What time did you tell Mom we'd be back?"

"Huh?"

"What time did you tell Mom we'd be back? You know, so she can send people to look for us when we don't show up?" Dave looked at the ground. "You did tell Mom we were going hunting, right? And where we were going, and what time we'd be back? You did that, right?"

"You know your mom doesn't like to wake up early. I didn't want to bother her."

"We are so boned."

"Don't be such a baby." Dave turned in a circle, surveying the land. "I've hunted all over these mountains. If I can just get out of these thick trees and find a landmark, I can walk us out of here, no problem." Looking back at the wreck, crushed against the huge pine, his eyes lit up. "Got it. Son, you just shin up that tree there, and see what you can see from the top. You should have a view for miles around."

"Like hell." Joe eyed the sap-crusted pillar. "The top must be a hundred feet up."

"Son, have I ever told you the story of the time your mom and I were in Hawaii, and we ate from a little stand that sold something called a pukka dog? And I tried to order a Coke, but they only had lemonade…"

"All *right*. I'm going, I'm going!" Standing on the Suburban to reach the lowest limb, Joe began to climb, because the only thing he'd heard more times than the king of France story was the pukka dog story.

He climbed higher and higher, until the thinning branches would no longer support his weight. The clouds had lifted, and he could see the valley floor for miles around. There was nothing, no landmarks, just the tops of trees, the lowering sky, and the wall of mountains in the distance.

He was just preparing to climb down again when his nose caught the faint, acrid scent of distant smoke. Heart in his throat, he risked climbing a little bit higher, straining his eyes across the valley. There, just where the mountains sloped down into the trees, was a wisp of gray twisting up towards the sky! Almost invisible in the mist, it was nonetheless real, a beacon of salvation. Half climbing, half-falling, Joey tumbled back to earth. "Dad! There's people here! I saw a fire, over that way, not too far!"

"Good spot, kid!" While Joey was climbing, Dave had extracted their backpacks and rifles from the crushed car, along with a few boxes of ammo. "Let's hurry, it's getting late." They shouldered their gear and hastened off in the direction of the smoke.

The trees began to thin as they progressed through the woods, seeming to adhere to some kind of strange order. One long strip was bare of vegetation altogether, and Joe and Dave followed this, as it went in the direction of the smoke.

"Son," said Dave, "this may be crazy, but I'll be damned if this isn't some kind of road."

"I think you're right, Dad. Look up there." Joey pointed ahead, where large, rectangular shapes loomed out of the mist. Buildings.

"Hey, we're saved!" The pair hastened forward, a new spring in their step.

As they drew closer, though, they slowed, then halted. Dave's jaw dropped. Joe stared. This was not a cluster of small backwoods cabins. They were standing at one end of what was clearly the main street of what was clearly a tidy, well-kept little town. Smoke curled from the chimneys of several neat houses, arranged along a street swept clean of snow. Some of the buildings appeared to be stores, with goods arranged behind shining glass windows. Apart from music tinkling from a bar at the end of the street, the whole place was completely silent.

"Should we knock on a door?" whispered Joe. "It doesn't look like anyone's out."

"It was like this back when I conquered France; we need to impress the natives. Let me handle it." Dave unslung his rifle and chambered a round. "Been awhile since I was king of anything." He aimed the muzzle into the air and fired. "HAIL TO THE CHIEF, BABY!"

Crack! Crack! Crack! A volley of return fire whizzed past their ears, pitting the side of the building behind them. Joe and Dave dived for cover, rolling behind a pile of stacked wood. "Shit! The bastards are armed!" cried Dave

"Dad, we're in Montana! Everybody is armed!" From beyond the woodpile came the unmistakable sounds of reloading. A second volley sent splinters flying.

"Hold your fire!" bellowed an unseen voice. Joe and Dave could hear bolts sliding and shotguns being racked, but there were no more shots. "You behind the woodpile! Throw down your guns and come out!"

"Like hell," said Dave, fumbling in his pocket for more ammo.

"For fuck's sake, Dad," Joe grabbed Dave's rifle and slid it out into the open, followed by his own. He stood and walked slowly round the woodpile, hands over his head. "Sorry about that, folks. My dad's a little senile." He twirled a finger by his ear to illustrate.

The man facing them did not seem impressed. In his mid-forties, rifle tucked under his arm, he looked like Al Capone, if Al Capone had been gnawed extensively by muskrats. His broad-shouldered pinstriped suit was shabby and frayed, the short, wide tie spotted with grease. A dingy fedora drooped over one eye. Joe tried again.

"My name's Joe, Joe Koontz. This is my dad, Dave."

"You might remember me from when I was the king of France," piped Dave, who had risen and joined Joe in the street.

"France." The man narrowed his eyes. "Never heard of it." He seemed to consider a long while. "Reckon he does look pretty bojangles, at that."

"What?"

"Bojangles. Nerts. Goofy. Off the wall."

"Oh, you mean crazy. Yeah, he's totally crazy. Mostly harmless, though."

"Hey," said Dave.

The man still looked unconvinced. "What's your business here?"

"We're lost. Our car went over a cliff across the valley, and we've been walking and walking. If we could just use your phone, we could call home and be out of your hair in a jiffy."

"Ain't no telephone." The man's jaw worked, and he spat in the snow at Joe's feet.

"Oh, off the grid, are you? Well, maybe we could borrow one of those cars and drive out once the weather clears. We'd give it a wash and a tune-up before we brought it back to you." Joe nodded at one of the tarp-draped vehicles parked in a yard.

"Cars don't leave the town." The man regarded them with a dispassionate gaze. As he stared, Joe became aware that a half-dozen other men had broken cover and joined him. They were dressed in similarly odd clothing; some wore suspenders, a few had flat cloth caps, others sported assorted felt bowlers and fedoras.

"Well, look, what do you suggest? We can't just stay here forever."

The man laughed, a short, sharp bark. "If we can, you can."

"No, seriously, I'm sure we can make it worth your while." Joe dug in his pockets. "I've got, let's see fourteen dollars and sixty-seven cents. Dad, you got any cash on you?" There was no reply. "Dad?" Joe looked over his shoulder to see Dave trotting back towards the woods, trundling as fast as his legs would take him.

"Hey, what's that crazy jerk think he's doing? Chester, stop him!" One of the men shoved his gun at another and gave chase down the road. Dave, sensing pursuit, put on an extra burst of speed, but alas, he was built more for fishing than for sprinting, and Chester tackled him just before he reached the woods. They rolled in the snow, punching and biting.

"Chester, the border! Don't get too close!" screamed the man. As they rolled towards the trees, there came a terrific cracking sound and a blinding flash of light. Joe fell to the ground and curled into a tight ball.

Little by little, the ringing in his ears faded. He uncurled experimentally, testing his limbs, fingers and toes. Everything seemed to still be attached. Levering up onto his knees, he looked around. The man who had questioned them was standing over him. He extended a hand. "You all right, son? That was a close one. Your pa was almost a goner." Behind the man, Joe saw Dave on his feet, wiping soot from his face with a handkerchief. His hair stood on end as if he'd been electrocuted; Chester stood beside him, looking identically frazzled.

Joe let the man help him to his feet. "Who *are* you? What *is* this place?" He was still in shock.

"Name's Bob. Bob Mann." The mysterious stranger gestured to the town with a sweep of his arm. "Welcome to Shelby."

They were in the living room of Bob Mann's house, sipping coffee brewed by Bob's wife, Zelda. Bob, tie loosened, lounged on a divan, sipping a gin and tonic. "Want one of these, boys?" he offered. "This is the good stuff we used to get from Canada, not like that stuff you get at the speakeasies. That shit'll make you go blind." He swigged deeply.

"Um, no thanks. You said you were going to tell us a story? Or at least what the hell is going on?"

"What's going on. Right. Where to begin." Bob sipped reflectively. "You remember the big fight between Dempsey and Gibbons in '23?"

Blank looks.

"Jack Dempsey? Tommy Gibbons? Two of the premier boxers of the 20th century? Any of that ring a bell?" Dave and Joe shook their heads. Bob sighed and held his glass out for a refill. "Okay. So, back in 1922, some guys discovered oil under the countryside around Shelby. Woop woop, everyone's excited, we're all gonna get rich, all kinds of people are gonna start coming in on the next train. The town fathers decide that with all this new income, Shelby is gonna become the Monte Carlo of northern Montana. World-class type of thing, tourists and socialites and high rollers every which way you look. And they decide that the first thing this new posh resort town needs is an arena. Big one, for all the huge shows and sporting events they're gonna have, once the oil people start showing up.

"So they buy up old Ed Miller's farm just west of town, and they build themselves the biggest, shiniest, most luxurious arena you ever saw. And get this, for the very first event, they get Dempsey to agree to fight Gibbons in this shiny new venue. Had to pay the fighters a bundle in advance, but it was OK, they were gonna make it back and then some, even if they did have to raise the ticket prices a little.

"The fight was scheduled for Independence Day, 1923." Bob stared into space for a moment before continuing. "It was a disaster. Turns out not that many people were willing to ride a train for a week to some dumpy little mountain town and then shell out big bucks to see a fight, even if it did feature Jack Dempsey. The organizers ended up giving away more than half the tickets for free. Between the cost of the arena and the fighters' advances, it ended up bankrupting the town. Oil dried up soon after. *Finis.*" Bob drained his drink. "We didn't even get to see a knockout."

"We?" Joe furrowed his brow. "Surely you aren't–"

Bob shifted to look blearily at Joe. "Old enough to have been there? You bet I am. Let's see, what year is it now?"

"2016."

"And I was born in 1880, which makes me, let's see, one hundred and thirty-six years old. Though I was forty-three when the fight happened." Bob settled back in his chair and closed his eyes.

"Hey!" Joe grabbed Bob by the arms and shook him like an infant. "You don't get to drop that on us and then just pass out! Finish the damn story!"

"Oh, all right, if you insist." Bob yawned. "Where was I?"

"At the part where you're immortal."

"Not immortal, just stuck in time." Bob got up and prodded the fire, sending sparks whirling up the chimney. "Look, let's back up a bit. You know Zeus? King of the gods?"

"Of course." Everyone in Montana knew Zeus. "Lives on top of Mount Olympus, over in Glacier National Park. What about him?"

"That's right. Well, as you may or may not know, old Zeus has a gambling problem. Specifically, he compulsively bets on sporting events. And he's really, really bad at it. He's lost millions upon millions over the centuries, but he just can't help himself. And of course, what with Glacier being just up the road from Shelby, of course he heard about the Dempsey-Gibbons fight as soon as it was announced. And of course, he bet big. On Gibbons."

"I'm guessing that Gibbons lost."

"That he did. And so did Zeus, big time." Bob had turned and was gazing into the fire, talking as much to himself as to Joe and Dave. "Turns out the king of the gods, despite considerable practice at it, isn't a very good loser. He blamed the town for hyping up the fight; thought we should have picked a more even matchup." He blew out his cheeks. "So, while we were sitting in the wreckage counting our lost money, old Zeus put a curse on us. He pulled the whole town, buildings and people and all, right out of time."

Bob turned again to look at Joe and Dave. "In Shelby, it's still 1923, and it always will be. Physically, we're still in Montana, but we're inside a bubble where time doesn't progress in a straight line. Everything that was in here when Zeus cursed us remains; we still have food and electricity and clothing, but we don't age, we don't die, and we can never leave. You saw what happens to those who try to cross the border."

Dave ran a hand over his scorched hair. "They get fried?"

"Like a convict sitting in Old Sparky." The fire was dying now, and Bob Mann's words came to them out of the shadows. "Every few years, someone wanders in from outside and gets trapped here. Not for long, though; somehow, the damn fools always think that they can sneak past the border. Me, though, I'm smart. I'm staying put, even if it means forever." The last embers vanished in the ashes. "We'll try to sort out some kind of permanent accommodations for you in the morning. Good night." In the darkness, Bob shuffled off down the hall.

Silence, except for the ticking of the clock over the mantel. After a while, Dave began to snore, but Joe sat awake in an armchair, watching a patch of moonlight make its way across the floor. He sat and sat, turning the situation over in his mind. Finally, as the first rays of dawn broke through the kitchen window and Dave began to stir on the sofa, he spoke, very low, a single word:

"Rematch."

"I'm not listening to this," said Bob Mann, getting up from the breakfast table. "Outsiders always have some crazy scheme for getting over the border, and they always, *always* end up getting burned alive. I am *not* getting involved with this."

"Just hear me out," pleaded Joe. "I'm not talking about a plan to sneak over the border, I'm talking about a way to lift the border for good. Make it disappear. Free us all."

Bob rolled his eyes. "You think you're the first one to try and get the curse lifted? Believe me, we tried everything. We begged, we apologized, we even offered to pay off the money that Zeus lost on the fight. No dice."

"Right, because it was never about the money to Zeus. It's all about the rush, don't you see, the excitement he feels when he wins a bet, or the despair when he loses. If you want to uncurse this place, you're going to have to help him get that adrenaline rush, that exhilaration again. And for that, we're going to need another fight."

"A rematch, you said. But even if we did agree to have another fight, how would that ever happen? Dempsey and Gibbons have to have been dead for years by now!"

"Not Dempsey and Gibbons. I'm talking about an even bigger rematch." Joe paused, dramatically. "I'm talking about Fury and Klitschko."

"Who the fuck are Fury and Klitschko?" Bob tried to scoff and drink orange juice at the same time and ended up choking. Dave pounded him on the back until he could breathe again. "Thanks, Dave. Now, once more, who the fuck–"

Joe held up a hand to silence him. "Tyson Fury and Wladimir Klitschko. Two of the greatest fighters of our time. Last year, they had a huge bout in Germany, which Fury won, causing Klitschko to vow revenge in the rematch. Only there was no rematch; it got postponed a couple of times, then Fury got in trouble with the officials, vacated his titles, and retired from boxing without ever fighting Klitchsko again."

Bob was listening intently now. "Go on."

"Well, if Zeus thinks that Fury is coming out of retirement and the rematch is back on, he won't be able to resist betting on it. And if he wins, he'll be so completely stoked…"

"…that he'd lift the curse for sure." Bob finished. He furrowed his brow. "But how are we going to fake a high-stakes boxing match out here in a time bubble in the middle of nowhere? And more importantly, how are we going to be sure that Zeus picks the winner?"

Joe winked and threw his arm around Dave, who wasn't expecting it and nearly face-planted into his breakfast. "You just leave that to me, Bob. I've got a plan."

The very next day, Zeus was perusing the racing form and jotting down the morning line odds in his living room atop Mount Olympus. Now, children, if you've ever been in a god's living room, you know that to them, the earth appears as a miniature scene at their feet, kind of like a really cool model train set, and they can zoom in on any area at will. It's actually pretty neat. Anyway, it was that way in the living room of Zeus that fine morning, when a sudden flurry of motion, not far from Mount Olympus, caught the god's eye. He set down his pencil and racing form and leaned forward to see better.

Down on the main street of Shelby, a newsboy was running, a sheaf of papers under his arm, one copy waved aloft, shouting, "Extra! Extra! Fury coming out of retirement for rematch with Klitschko! Klitschko heavily favored to win!"

People crowded round to buy the papers; as the copies were distributed, they stood in groups in the street, talking at unusually loud volumes. "WHY, I NEVER! FURY COMING OUT OF RETIREMENT AND COMING HERE TO FIGHT THE REMATCH WITH KLITSCHKO? THAT'S BIG NEWS!" bellowed a woman, turning her body to project towards Mount Olympus.

"IT CERTAINLY IS, MABEL! AND I HEAR THAT THE ODDS ON FURY ARE REALLY LONG RIGHT NOW. IF YOU WERE TO BET ON HIM AND HE WON, YOU WOULD STAND TO MAKE A BUNDLE!" Chester paused and consulted the script hidden in his paper. "SAY, MAYBE I'LL TRY TO GET SOME OF THAT ACTION. I HEARD THAT FURY'S BEEN TRAINING NONSTOP FOR THIS FIGHT."

"DID YOU REALLY?" put in another man, cupping his hands around his mouth and shouting towards the mountain. "WELL, I HEARD THAT KLITSCHKO HASN'T REALLY RECOVERED FROM THE LAST FIGHT, AND HE'S

NOT BEEN PERFORMING AS WELL AS USUAL WITH HIS SPARRING PARTNERS."

"WOW, THAT'S REALLY SOMETHING!" screamed Chester, his voice beginning to go hoarse. "TELL YOU WHAT, DON'T TELL ANYONE ELSE WHAT YOU JUST TOLD ME. IF WE GO TO THE BOOKIES RIGHT NOW, I BET WE CAN GET A HUNDRED TO ONE ON FURY!"

"OK!" yelled the second man.

"OK!" shrieked the woman. They all bustled off together down the street. Up on Mount Olympus, Zeus grabbed his telephone and began to dial Big Eddie, the bookie of the gods.

Fast-forward one week. The arena at the edge of town glittered with every light bulb in Shelby; the rest of the town was dark and silent. Martial music blared; on the marquee, ten-foot tall letters proclaimed: FURY VS KLITSCHKO II: THE RE-PUNCHENING. Inside, the crowd was thick, filling almost all the seats, making enough noise to raise the roof. If you had inspected the crowd closely, you might have noticed that it was largely made up of dressed-up lawn statues, department store mannequins, and even a few logs wearing hats, and that the noise was coming from a few phonographs positioned strategically around the arena. But if you weren't paying too much attention, it could just about pass.

Down in the locker rooms, Dave was adjusting his black toupee, which kept sliding down over his eyes. "Why do I have to be Klitschko?" he grumbled. "Stupid Ukrainians with their stupid funny names. I want to be Fury instead."

"I told you, Dad," replied Joe, applying extra glue to his false beard. "It was my idea, so I get to be the guy with the cool name. End of story."

"My trunks don't fit right, either." Dave shimmied, trying to settle the elastic around his belly."

"Look, just remember, at the end of the third round, that's when you take your dive. OK?"

"Fine, fine." Dave discovered that he couldn't pick out a wedgie while wearing boxing gloves and sighed heavily. "Let's get this show on the road."

"OK, then. Ready when you are, Bob."

Bob Mann, in short sleeves and a referee's bow tie, was sweating profusely. "This is insane," he muttered, shoving open the locker room door and striding towards the ring in the center of the arena, Joe and Dave tagging after him like puppies.

They parted the ropes and climbed into the ring, Joe and Dave splitting to their corners, Bob remaining in the middle. He raised his arms, saluting the fake crowd. "LADIEEEEEEES AND GENTLEMEN! WELCOME TO THE REMATCH WE'VE ALL BEEN WAITING FOR! IN THIS CORNER, FIGHTING OUT OF LONDON, ENGLAND, NEWLY OUT OF RETIREMENT, TYSON FURY!" Joe leaped into the middle of the ring, pumping his arms. The crowd roared on the phonographs. "AND IN THIS CORNER, FIGHTING OUT OF KIEV, UKRAINE, AND LOOKING FOR VENGEANCE, WLADIMIR

KLITSCHKO!" Dave juked left and right, punching the air. He and Joe advanced to the center of the ring and circled each other, glowering.

"All right, gentlemen, I want a good, clean fight. No hitting below the belt, and protect yourselves at all times." Then, *sotto voce*, "Don't screw this up." Bob chopped his hand between them. "FIGHT!"

Dave and Joe crouched and circled. Dave swung first, a wild blow that missed Joe entirely and sent him careening into the ropes under his own momentum. "Dad, focus!" Joe hissed. "I'm over here!"

"Well, you shouldn't have made me take off my glasses for this. I can't see a thing." Overhead, thunder rumbled. Zeus was watching.

They bopped each other ineffectually a few times, shuffling and tripping, until a white-faced Bob rang the bell for the end of the round. Joe retreated to his corner and swigged water from a bottle. In his corner, Dave gulped from a pint of gin he'd swiped from Bob's house and hidden under his chair. Joe shot him a look that said *Really?* Dave shot back a look that said *What? A guy can't have a drink when he's stressed?*

It was a much looser Dave that strutted back out for round two. "Wassa matter, boy?" he taunted. "Can't take the heat?" He slugged Joe hard in the breadbasket, and Joe oofed to the ground. Dave pounced, throwing haymakers, landing about half of them.

"Ring the bell, Bob! Ring the bell!" Joe screamed, covering his head. *Clang!* The round ended just in time.

"OK, change of plans." Joe muttered as he got to his feet. "First thing next round is when you go down, OK, Dad?" Dave grinned. "OKAY, Dad?"

"Oh, sure." Dave giggled and danced back to his corner and his gin.

Third round. Joe stomped out of his corner, determined to end it before Dave could start any more mischief. He swung hard for Dave's nose, but Dave evaporated, juking left and dancing on the balls of his feet. "*Woo hoo hoooooo!*" he crowed.

Joe tried a left hook followed by a right cross, but again, Dave dodged, ducking around Joe. He leaped onto Joe's back like a monkey, wrapping arms and legs around his neck and waist.

"Dad, ow! Get off, we're supposed to be boxing!" Dave hooted and tightened his grip. Bob Mann paced around the pair, brow furrowed, unsure what to do. If he stopped the fight now, Zeus wouldn't win his bet, and they would remain trapped in Shelby forever.

He needn't have worried. Bit by bit, like a girl getting out of a too-tight dress, Joe worked Dave down towards the canvas, wriggling and shimmying until he was almost sitting down in the center of the ring. With a final heave, he broke Dave's grip and, like a panther wearing boxing trunks, dropped down on top of him, pinning him to the ground. Dave thrashed and flailed, struggling to get free. "Bob, the count! I can't hold him for long!" yelled Joe.

"Onetwothreefourfivesixseveneightnineten!"   Bob drummed the heel of his hand on the canvas. "That's it!" He grabbed Joe's left arm, hoisting him to his feet, and raised his glove into the air. "LADIES AND GENTLEMEN, THE WINNER BY TECHNICAL KNOCKOUT AND STILL CHAMPION, TYSON FURY!" With his free hand, Joe tried to subtly pat his false beard, which had come partly unglued, back into place. The phonograph crowd roared approval. Overhead, the godly thunder rumbled again.

"I lost?" Dave, lying on the canvas, looked crestfallen.

"There's a first time for everything, Dad. Come on, let's head for home." Joe helped his father up, and with a final wave to the stands, they jumped through the ropes and bolted for the locker room.

They changed hurriedly and hustled out the side door, running towards the main street where the townspeople had assembled, suitcases packed and cars loaded. Chester, standing on the running board of an old pickup truck, hailed them as they drew near. "That was too god damn close for comfort, Bob. Do you think it worked?"

"We'll know in a minute." Bob tossed a set of keys to Joe. "Here, you drive." He scurried around to the passenger side, while Dave piled into the back. Joe, behind the wheel, turned the key; the engine caught, and slowly, headlights dim in the dark night, the convoy crept out of town.

They approached the border where Dave had nearly been incinerated the day they arrived in Shelby. Bob, in the front seat, had his eyes shut tight and was muttering Hail Marys under his breath. Joe took a single deep inhale and blew out hard. "All right, then. Here we go." With a wrench, he kicked the car into high gear, stomped on the accelerator, and gunned it toward the border at top speed.

The old car surged forward, faster and faster towards the trees. The snowbanks on either side flew by as they accelerated, until with a strangled scream from Bob, they punched over the border and down the forest road.

And nothing happened.

Bob peeked through his fingers. "We're out?" He checked the rearview mirror; a parade of headlights trailed after them. "We're out! We're out!" Joe whooped and pounded on the steering wheel; behind them, car horns honked jubilantly. Bob settled back in his seat, a grin stretching from ear to ear. "We're out. We're really out."

"Welcome to the twenty-first century, Bob." Joe was grinning, too. "First thing we gotta do when we get home, is get you some new clothes. And a cell phone. You don't have to decide now, but just start considering: do you want to be an iPhone guy or an Android guy?"

The only response was a strangled hiss from the passenger side. Coming out of a sharp turn, Joe glanced over to see Bob, now sitting bolt upright, beginning to wrinkle, then shrivel, as ninety-three years of suspended time suddenly crashed into his body. When you are older, children, I will let you watch *Indiana Jones and the Last Crusade*, and you will have a good idea of what happened to Bob Mann, but until then, you will just have to imagine it. Bob's cheeks hollowed, his eyes sank in, and his flesh wasted away on his bones. In a matter of seconds, all that was left of Bob was a pile of dust and some ratty old clothing. From the road behind came the sound of crunching metal and breaking glass, as a dozen vintage automobiles, suddenly driverless, plunged off the road, down embankments, and into trees.

"Huh." said Dave, peering into the front seat. "If only there had been some way to predict that that would happen."

"There was no way of knowing." Joe adjusted the rearview mirror. "But look on the bright side, we should be home in time for breakfast."

"Hallelujah." Dave scrambled over the seat, dusting the remains of Bob Mann onto the floor so that he could take shotgun. Alone on the road, the vintage sedan wended its way towards Missoula. And that children, is how your Uncle Joey and Grandpa Dave found (and lost again) the Lost City of Shelby.

THE END

How Joe Got His Super Powers

This story, children, begins as so many stories about your Uncle Joe do, with Joe waking up on the floor of a roadside motel room, with little to no recollection of how he got there.

Groggily, he rolled over onto one side and surveyed the environment. Empty Pringles cans and squashed gummy bears littered the carpet. There was a smear of something green and sticky on the ceiling. Up on the stripped bed, a hairy mound shifted, and empty bottles clanked. *Well, at least I've found Bridger*, thought Joe, blearily. Inch by inch, he levered himself upright until he was sitting up against the box spring, legs spraddled in front of him. He reached up and back to thump Bridger in the belly. "Bridger. Dude. Wake up."

"Hrnk?" Bridger logrolled off the bed, nearly crushing Joe. He blinked in the feeble light filtering through the motel curtains. He was nude. I mean, of course he was. He's Bridger.

"Shit, man, we must have really had a party last night. I think we might have ended up somewhere savage, like maybe North Dakota."

By now Bridger was also sitting up, rubbing his eyes. "You *wish* we were in North Dakota. Pretty sure we're still in Canada."

"Ha! Canada!" Joe nearly laughed, but the sudden realization sobered him in an instant. They *were* in Canada.

Now, you may have learned in school that there is no such place as Canada, that it's only a story made up to scare children. But schools don't know everything, and the fact is that Canada is very real, though it is hard to reach, and almost impossible to return from, at least for most people. Those who do return speak of strange, pale natives who are oddly polite to strangers and worship a god named Tim Horton.

People who go to Canada rarely do so on purpose. Instead, they say, they get lost inside the swirling mists that perpetually shroud the border, and after a long, foggy walk, they suddenly emerge into open air, smelling faintly of maple

136

syrup. Often, they do not know how far astray they've gone, until they stumble upon a pickup hockey game; for you see, Canadians, unless you look closely, appear exactly the same as you or I. Only upon close inspection do you notice their beaverlike tails, or their hair that is actually thousands of tiny maple leaves, or the fact that they each have a second head that sits just behind their regular head and occasionally makes pithy remarks.

It was so with Joe and Bridger, who, on that fateful night, became catastrophically lost while trying to get from Katie O'Keefe's to the Fox Club (Bridger was driving). The road twisted and turned, and in the fog they narrowly avoided hitting a bear (don't laugh, children, for bears are as real as Canada). By the time Bridger admitted he was lost, it was too late: the mist had evaporated, the road home had disappeared, and they were left alone in the moonlight. In the stillness, a distant pack of Canadians set up their melancholy chorus of "Sorry!"

None of this, of course, quite explained how Joe and Bridger came to be in this desolate motel amid the wreckage of a junk food binge, but being the intrepid boys they were, they resolved to puzzle it out. "First things first," observed Bridger, rolling onto all fours and bear-crawling towards the bathroom. "Potty break, then evaluate the situation."

Joe covered his eyes. "Could you put some shorts on somewhere in there?"

"I don't tell *you* how to live." Bridger used the counter to haul himself to his feet and disappeared into the bathroom. A moment later: "Joe? You got a minute? Need a quick hallucination check in here."

Joe wobbled upright. "Be right there, buddy." A couple of staggers later, he had joined Bridger in the bathroom.

"See, what I'm seeing is a huge black dog in the bathtub."

"Mm-hm. Mm-hm." Joe rubbed his chin.

"Got some glowing red eyes there."

"I see 'em."

"Lots of teeth."

"Seems friendly, though." True, the enormous, fanged, red-eyed beast in the tub was wagging its bushy tail, paws the size of catcher's mitts propped on the porcelain edge. "First thing we should do is, we should check for tags."

"OK then. Get on with it."

"I'm more of a cat person." Joe eyed the dog cautiously.

"Well, I'm naked."

"OK, fine. Just don't remind me of that again." Joe sidled forward. "Hey there. Hey, doggie." The immense tail thumped against the soap dish. Joe slowly extended his hand. "Easy, there, that's a good dog." The hound stretched out its neck, sniffed twice, then delicately licked Joe's hand with a giant pink tongue.

"Easy, boy, easy." Joe spotted his belt slung over the towel bar above the tub. Stroking the dog's ears with one hand, he slowly reached up and snagged it. "That's it. Good boy," he cooed, looping the belt around its massive neck to form a crude leash. "Let's go. Out of the tub, now." He backed towards the door; obediently, the dog heaved itself up and over the porcelain rim to follow him, splashing tepid water across the floor. Gently tugging the leash, Joe guided the giant hound out into the room.

Bridger had opened the drapes and acquired some shorts, not necessarily in that order, and in the morning light, they were able to inspect the mighty animal. He was immense, as long as a kayak from the tip of his snuffling nose to the end of his brushy tail. Even in the light, his red eyes still glowed against his pitch-black coat; the morning sun glistened on a streamer of drool that dripped from one of his saberlike fangs. The huge shoulders and haunches seemed to fill the room, and the tail thumped loudly against the bureau as the beast inspected its new environment.

About the hound's neck, Bridger observed a gleam of metal. Moving gingerly, he bent to examine it. "Joe, he's got a collar on," he called.

"Awesome. Does it have an address on it?" The dog was snuffling through the detritus of last night's binge; it threw back its head to gulp down a can of Pringles. For real, it ate the can and everything.

"Nope, looks like just a name." Bridger turned the collar so the nameplate was illuminated. In a strange and angular script, it was engraved with a single word: SHUKI.

"Shuki?" Bridger wondered aloud. The dog arfed happily. "Is that your name, buddy? Shuki?" The massive tail thumped as Shuki wriggled from end to end. Bridger turned to Joe. "He says his name's Shuki."

"Fantastic. What does he say we should do now?"

"Shuki? Any insight?" The hound woofed again. "Shuki says we should go get breakfast."

Joe blew out his cheeks. "Sure. He ate all our snacks anyway. Let's go see what we can find in this godforsaken Canadian wasteland."

Loading Shuki into the car was no easy feat, but they managed it; the dog filled the entire backseat, his tail hanging out one window, his head out the other. As Joe eased the car out of the motel parking lot and headed down the highway, Shuki turned his face into the breeze and chuffled with joy.

They had not gone far when Bridger pointed at a clearing up ahead. "Look, there's one of those temples we passed on the way in. I bet the monks would give us something to eat." Indeed, there was a squat, low-slung temple building beside the road; the lights were on, and figures could be seen moving behind the windows. Over the door, the sacred script of TIM HORTON'S glowed with holy light. Joe steered the car to the shoulder and parked.

"Come on, Shuki. Time for donuts," said Bridger, opening the rear door.

"He's coming?"

"Well, we can't leave him in the car. He'll overheat."

"Fair enough." Crossing to the temple door, Joe pushed it open; they were greeted by a rush of warm air. Scenting food, Shuki shoved ahead of the two friends and entered first.

At first no one noticed them, the congregants sitting bowed over their tables. At the sound of giant doggy toenails clicking across the floor, however, an old man in the corner looked up, registered Shuki padding towards the counter, and screamed. "IT'S BLACK SHUCK!"

The room exploded. People dived under tables and fled out the doors. The plate glass window shattered as a desperate couple leaped through it and landed in the bushes out front. Amid the commotion, shrieks rang out: *It's Black Shuck! Run for your lives! Old Shuck! Don't look at him!* Within seconds, the temple was deserted.

"Well, shit." Joe surveyed the wreckage; food and crockery were littered all around. "I don't think we're going to get any breakfast here."

"Sheesh, everyone runs away screaming and you just give up? Let's have a look around." Bridger began to poke through the debris. Across the room, Shuki had snuffled over to the counter along the far wall. Heaving his front paws onto the countertop, he peered over the edge, then threw back his head and let loose a bone-chilling howl. "There, you see? Shuki found something. Good boy, Shuki, good boy!" The dog's eyes glowed red at the praise.

Joe shrugged and vaulted the counter, Bridger tumbling and rolling after. At first, they could not tell what Shuki had been howling at, but in a moment, a stifled whimper directed them to a pile of rags huddled under the counter, which, after a brisk prodding, revealed itself to be a shivering, khaki-clad monk.

"Mister Odin sir how great to see you again I'm so sorry we've been behind in our tributes can I get you a cup of coffee and a donut maybe and we can work something out please oh please we're so sorry," the monk babbled through tears, clutching his ceremonial visor over his eyes.

"What," said Bridger.

Sniffling, the monk peeked out from underneath his visor to peer at Joe and Bridger, but at the sight of Shuki's giant paws hanging over the edge of the counter, he ducked back under and resumed sobbing. "Mister Odin sir it's so great to see you here I really love the human forms you and your friend have chosen this time please don't let Shuck eat me sir pleeeeeeease."

"This is getting us nowhere," said Joe.

"Hang on," said Bridger. He reached out to place a palm on the back of the monk's head, gently pressing his chin to his chest, revealing the secondary head that all Canadians keep stashed behind their main head. This head was bald, with piercing blue eyes that looked calmly back at Bridger. "You got your head right, buddy?" Bridger asked.

"Yes, indeed," replied the head. Inexplicably, it had a British accent.

"Okay. We just got into town last night. When we woke up, we had this dog with us. We don't know who he belongs to or where he lives, but we'd really like to take him home. And maybe get some donuts."

The head blinked. "You really don't know? That, my unlucky friends, is Shukir, known around here as Black Shuck. He's Odin's war dog, and anyone who looks upon him is sure to die."

"He's *whose* war dog, now?"

"Oh for— what do they teach in American schools? Odin. Norse god of war and death. Lives just up the road in Valhalla."

"I thought that was in Montana."

"That's Mount Olympus you're thinking of, old chap."

"Oh, okay. So, what gives with your pal here?"

"This village is behind in their tributes to Valhalla. He's afraid that Odin in his wrath has sent Black Shuck to destroy us all." The monk, head still bowed, whimpered in agreement.

"Okay, then, to summarize: we've got ourselves a supernatural hellhound belonging to the Norse god of war who is pissed off at this village and we're all doomed to die."

"Precisely correct."

"And you said Valhalla is just up this road here?"

"Aboot an hour's drive."

"Okay. Thanks, buddy. We'll figure something out."

"Good luck, then." Bridger released the monk, and the secondary head tucked itself back down its host's collar. Bridger turned to Joe. "You thinking what I'm thinking?"

"Hey, if we're gonna die anyway…"

Ten minutes later, Shuki stuck his head out the car window and let the wind flap his ears as Joe gunned it down the road toward Valhalla.

"How will we know when we're getting close?" Bridger asked.

"Keep an eye on Shuki. I bet he'll let us know when he's close to home."

Sure enough, as Joe slowed to navigate a turn, Shuki yelped and strained his head farther out the window, wagging so hard that he dented the car's bodywork. "This way, buddy?" Joe had spotted a turning off the main road, almost hidden amongst the pines. Shuki yelped again in affirmation, and Joe swerved to guide the car up the unpaved track.

Though the sun was high, it was twilight in the forest; barely any light filtered through the boughs of the trees. Shuki was growing increasingly agitated. "Dude, let's let him out and see if he'll lead us," said Joe. Bridger reached back to pop open the rear door, and the hound leaped out, loping ahead of the car. Joe followed cautiously.

Finally, after one last turn, they came to an open, well-lit clearing. On the far side, in the shade of the pines, stood a small rectangular cabin with a railed porch along the front and a set of steps made from rough-hewn logs. On this porch, tipped back in a chair with his feet up on the railing, sat a stringy, sinewy old man in denim overalls and no shirt, absently staring up at the sky and humming an odd tune into his beard.

Shuki let out a single sharp bark and bounded towards the cabin. At the sound, the old man bolted upright, shouting across the clearing, "SHUKI! Here, boy, here!" In a moment, the hound was on the porch, up on his hind legs with his paws draped over the old man's shoulders, covering his face with ardent licks. Joe put the car in park, and he and Bridger both

148

exited and approached the cabin. "Mister Odin?" Joe called as they neared. "We found your dog. Can we be excused from death, please?"

Arms still wrapped around Shuki's neck, the old man looked over at the friends with barely concealed irritation. "Oh, you did, did you? You needn't have brought him back yourselves, you know. He can find his own way. Can't you, my good boy?" He rubbed the beast's ears vigorously, flopping them to and fro.

"Well, we just thought that if we explained that we're not from the village down there, and that we're not the ones stiffing you on your tributes, that maybe we could forget the whole look-at-the-dog-and-then-die thing."

"Shuki and I don't care about the tributes, nor is it fatal to look upon him, we just want the villagers to be too intimidated to wander up here. We like our privacy." Shuki had dropped down to all fours, and Odin had turned to fix the boys with an unfriendly gaze. "The rest of Valhalla is so rowdy all the time, what with the fighting all day and the feasting all night. Sometimes a god just wants a nice quiet place to relax.

A place *without* any visitors." The god of war and death glared at them.

"No visitors, right you are," said Joe, edging back towards the car. "If you can tell us how to get back to America, we'll be out of your hair in a jiffy."

Odin sighed. "Very well. I'll transport you back to your home if you promise never to return. Wait here, and I'll fetch my spear."

"Wait, what?" Joe tried to edge backward faster.

Bridger stepped forward. "Hold, up, your godliness," he said. "We still drove your dog all the way back here for you. He could have gotten hit by a car or trampled by a moose or mauled by a beaver. How about a little something, you know, for the trouble?"

"Dude, leave it alone. We've got a chance to go home, don't push it," Joe muttered. He twisted his fingers into the back of Bridger's shirt and tried to subtly pull him back towards the car.

Up on the porch, Odin opened his mouth as if to speak, then suddenly laughed out loud. "By my beard, so you did, and you shall have your reward. Wait here, lads, and I'll bring it straight away." He disappeared into the cabin's black interior.

Joe opened the car door, fumbling for the keys in his pocket. "Dude, get in. I got a bad feeling about this."

But it was too late. Odin was back out of the cabin and crossing the yard with Gungnir, the shining golden Spear of Heaven, propped on his left shoulder. Joe froze, his hand on the door handle. It took him a moment to realize that Odin was holding out two small white envelopes in his right hand. "Here you are lads, one for each of you. Your just rewards," the god boomed heartily. Bridger winked at Joe and selected an envelope; with numb fingers, Joe accepted the remaining one. "Now, then, time to send you home. Just close your eyes and count to three, and it will all be done." Joe squinched his eyes tight. "And a one, and a two, and a—"

Lightning flashed and thunder boomed. Joe had the sensation of being whirled through space, though he could see

151

nothing but blackness. He tried to scream, but the roaring wind whipped his voice away. He was sure that this was the end.

And then, suddenly, it was over. The wind ceased, the noise quieted, and through his closed eyelids, Joe sensed the glow of sunlight. Opening his eyes, he found himself standing beside the car, on the shoulder of a wide country road. Sunshine was beaming down softly, and a pair of swallows rode the gentle breeze through the waving saplings beside the pavement.

"Is this Heaven?" Joe whispered. If it was, then clearly Saint Peter hadn't gotten a look at his complete file.

"No, dude, it's I-90. We must be just east of town." Bridger had found the emergency bottle of Hot Damn under the passenger seat, and he gestured with the bottleneck towards the green highway sign that read: MISSOULA 5 MILES.

Joe's shoulders sagged with relief. "We did it. We're home." He never wanted to go to Canada again. "Let's go,

Bridger. Supper's waiting." The boys got back into the car, and Joe set a course for Missoula.

From the pocket of his jeans, Bridger pulled out the envelope that Odin had given him. "Wonder how much we got?" he mused, sticking a finger under the flap and ripping it open. He peered inside. "Hey, there's no money in here."

"You were expecting a Norse god to have envelopes of American cash just laying around?"

"Well, maybe…no, wait, there's a card in here. Maybe it's for Amazon." Bridger pulled out a cardboard rectangle and turned it over. On the reverse, in the same runic script as on Shuki's collar, was written the words: *BURP FIRE*. Bridger frowned. "What the shit? Does yours say something crazy, too?"

"Check it and see," replied Joe, fishing his envelope out and passing it across. Bridger ripped it open and extracted the card. The script on the back read: *REPEL ELEPHANTS*. "Huh," said Joe.

Bridger had his phone out and was Googling intently. "Hang on, there's got to be more here than meets the eye." He tapped a few more times. "Says here on Wikipedia that Odin has the ability to bestow super powers on mortals. Some of the powers are epic, others are useless. But sometimes, the powers end up destroying the people who wield them." He swigged more Hot Damn nervously.

"Don't worry about it, dude. He's just messing with our heads to make sure we don't come back."

"Yeah, you're probably right. I'm sure there's nothing to worry ab–UUUURRRRRRRPPPP!" A jet of flames shot out of Bridger's open mouth as he belched, melting a hole in the windshield.

"Oh my God, dude!" yelled Joe, struggling to keep the car steady.

"I'm sorry!" wailed Bridger. "It's Odin's curse!" He gulped Hot Damn to quench the burn in his mouth.

"No, Bridger, no more liquor!"

"Why no–UUUUUUURRRRRRRPPPP!" The next blast melted the radio.

"Out the window, man, out the window!" Bridger rolled down the passenger side and incinerated a stand of pine they were driving past.

"Hang in there, buddy. We'll get you home and figure a way to get this curse lifted." Joe floored it towards Missoula.

There was no traffic as they roared into town and pulled up in front of Joe's house. "Where is everyone?" whispered Bridger, carefully pointing his mouth in a safe direction.

Before Joe could reply, across the rooftops of Missoula there came a violent clanging sound, the frantic ringing of a dozen gigantic bells in unison. "The mammoth alarm!" Joe gasped.

As you know, children, up until fairly recently, downtown Missoula suffered from periodic raids by herds of rampaging woolly mammoths, which would topple buildings, destroy supplies, and generally ruin the tourist industry. It was just such a raid that was occurring as the boys arrived in town, and judging by the panicked cries issuing from downtown, it appeared to be even worse than usual.

All able-bodied Missoulians were expected to rally to the downtown area in the event of a mammoth attack, so Joe and Bridger sprinted at top speed towards the sounds of the commotion, Bridger pausing to flame-burp a dumpster. The fighting was fiercest near the carousel in the park, where the townspeople were holding the mammoths off with spears and clubs, but a few of the fearsome pachyderms had made their way up from the river bottom and into the entertainment district.

A terrorized pair of little girls cowered against the back wall of a candy shop as the front window shattered and a hairy trunk snaked inside, whooshing up spilled jellybeans from the shop floor. Nearer and nearer it came, the mammoth using its tusks to widen the hole and trample further and further inside. The girls shrieked aloud and pressed back against the wall.

A blinding green light flashed, and with an earsplitting bellow, the mammoth backed out of the candy shop, whirling to face a gangly redheaded woman in a robotic exoskeleton standing in the middle of the road—your Aunt Laura. "Run, girls!" she shouted. "I'll hold it off!" She blasted the mammoth again with her laser as the children scrambled out through the rubble and pelted off to safety.

Back at the scene of the battle, Joe skidded to a stop on the main street. Bridger ran up panting behind him, carrying a pair of spears. "I got one for you, Joe, here!"

Joe did not move.

"Joe! Take your spear before they come this way!" Bridger shoved the weapon at his friend.

Joe still did not move. His face felt hot. His palms itched. Up the street, a pair of huge mammoths had noticed their presence, and with a deafening trumpet, they began to charge.

Joe could feel electricity running through his body. He seemed to be floating just above the ground; through the rushing sound in his ears, he could barely make out Bridger pleading with him to take the spear.

In seeming slow motion, the mammoths drew nearer and nearer. Slowly, stately, Joe raised his arms above his head, and in a thunderous voice that Bridger had never heard before, he bellowed, *"MAMMOTHS, BEGONE!"*

Not ten yards away from Joe, the mammoths screeched to a halt. They swayed. They reeled. Then, trumpeting in alarm, they turned tail and fled. Joe strode after them, hands aloft as if in exorcism. *"MAMMOTHS, BEGONE!"*

Bridger goggled. From the river bottom, there were more honks and squeals from panicking mammoths and the sound of stampeding behemoths crashing back across the river. *"MAMMOTHS, BEGONE!"* Joe roared again. A ragged cheer went up from the waterfront as the last mammoth lumbered away into the forest. Joe blinked. He lowered his hands, staring. The lightning had left his eyes.

"Dude," Bridger breathed. "You can repel *all kinds* of elephants."

Joe laughed in disbelief. "Holy shit."

From the wrecked shops and restaurants, people were pouring into the street. They chanted "JOE! JOE! JOE!" and lifted him onto their shoulders, beginning a parade towards the town square.

"Hey!" yelled Bridger, running along to keep pace. "Weren't we going to find me a doctor or something, for my problem?"

"Don't worry!" Joe called back. "I have an idea!"

"Oh, shit," said Bridger, taking another swig of Hot Damn.

Mid-morning in Valhalla. Odin was inside his cabin, heating a pot of coffee on his wood-burning stove. On the rug nearby, Shuki lay melting in a puddle of sunshine. The sun streamed down, warming the clearing, while the birds chirped in the trees. It was a good day to be a god.

Suddenly, Shuki bolted upright. Hackles bristling, he faced the door and growled low and deep. "What is it, my friend?" asked Odin, looking up as he stirred his coffee.

THUD! THUD! THUD! The ground beneath the cabin began to shake. Odin moved to stand in the doorway. From the forest came an angry trumpet and the sound of pine trees cracking and breaking, as the first mammoth came crashing into the clearing.

"No!" screamed Odin, waving his arms. "Get out of here, you filthy beasts! You're ruining my place! Scram!" The mammoth ignored him, milling about as more of his family came lumbering out of the trees.

"Is that any way to greet your old friends?" asked Joe, stepping out of the forest with his hands aloft, Bridger trailing behind. It had been difficult keeping the mammoth herd together through the mists of the Canadian border and up the highway to Valhalla, but by moving constantly, he had been able to keep them in a tight ball and moving in the right direction. "I believe we have an issue to resolve with my pal Bridger here."

Odin narrowed his eyes. "No take-backsies. You asked for the power, now you're stuck with it."

"Trade us, then," Joe challenged. "Take the fire burps and give him something he can live with. Otherwise, these mammoths are your new neighbors."

Odin hesitated. One of the mammoths raised its tail and took an immense shit in the center of the clearing. "All right!" the god screamed. "All right! Just take these foul creatures somewhere else!"

"Not until you un-curse Bridger."

"Jesus H. Christ on a stick." Odin turned and scuttled back into the cabin. In a minute he emerged with a fresh white envelope. He thrust it at Bridger. "Here! This should suit you fine!"

Bridger ripped the envelope open and pulled out the card. *IRON LIVER,* it read.

"Not so fast," said Bridger. "What's it mean?"

"It means you can eat and drink as much as you like and you won't die of liver failure," said Odin.

"And I won't burp fire anymore?"

'You won't burp fire anymore. Now, please, send these vile animals somewhere else!"

Joe turned, hands lifted. ***"MAMMOTHS, BEGONE!"*** The mammoths dispersed, trumpeting wildly, into the depths of Valhalla. He turned once more to face the king of the gods. "And now, Mister Odin sir, if you wouldn't mind fetching that fancy spear that sends us home…"

"Fine," said Odin. "Fucking fine."

And that, children, is why there are no more mammoths in Missoula.

THE END

How Renee and Lauren Saved the NFL

This is a different kind of tale than we usually tell here, children, for it is not a tale about Uncle Joey (though he will show up for a cameo later, I promise). No, this is a very special tale, about two brave little girls named Renee and Lauren, and how they rescued the entire National Football League from certain ruin.

It all began on a warm afternoon in late summer, not too long before dinner time. The girls were playing by themselves in the front yard of their house: Renee was drawing with colored chalk on the concrete driveway, while her little sister Lauren was catching grasshoppers in the tall grass nearby. Feeling the vibration of distant hoofbeats, Renee looked up from her drawing to see three riders on horseback, approaching the house in a cloud of dust. They carried no banner to identify themselves, but their dark brown robes silhouetted them against the setting sun, the hoods pulled over their heads, concealing their faces as they approached.

"Monks coming, Mom!" Renee hollered towards the house. Travelers often stopped at their house to ask food and shelter for the night, and Renee could usually tell apart the knights and monks and nobles and peasants, even at a distance.

The girls' mother appeared in the doorway, wiping her hands on a towel. "Sure enough. All right, when they get here, show them the way to the stables. I'll get the guest rooms ready." She vanished back into the house.

Lauren joined her sister at the foot of the driveway, waving as the monks approached. The leader pulled up his reins as he drew near, slowing his tall grey horse to a walk. "Good evening, young ladies," he intoned in a deep voice. "Might you have a place for three weary travelers, who have come many a difficult mile today?"

"Yep, we saw you coming a while ago," answered Renee. "Our mom's getting some rooms ready for you right now. She said for you to take your horses around back to the stables and put them up. Supper should be ready by the time you're done."

"I caught some grasshoppers!" chimed in Lauren, lifting her jar up for inspection.

"Most impressive. And many thanks, young ladies." The chief monk bowed. "With whom do I have the pleasure of speaking?"

"My name's Renee, and this is my little sister, Lauren."

"Renee and Lauren, we are pleased to make your acquaintance. I am Brother Richard, and my companions are Brother Kam and Brother Earl. With your kind permission, we'll join you indoors as soon as our horses are settled."

"See you soon!" The monks dismounted and led their steeds back towards the stables, and Renee and Lauren went inside to wash their hands before dinner.

The monks were pleasant and polite as they ate their dinners, their cowls still pulled over their heads. The girls, excused from the table, were playing a board game on the living room floor. "Delicious pork chops, Mrs. H," said Brother Richard, helping himself to seconds.

"The potatoes are exquisite," chimed in Brother Earl, also holding his plate out for another serving.

From the living room, Renee's voice rang out. "Hey, you only rolled a five, but you moved six places! Quit cheating, Tom Brady!"

"I'm not cheating! You're the one who's cheating, Bill Belichick!" retorted Lauren, balling up her tiny fists.

In the kitchen, three hooded heads swiveled to look at the girls, who had knocked over their game and were scuffling on the floor. As their mother swept in to break it up, Renee noticed that Brother Richard's eyes were shining out of the shadows of his cowl. "I take it that you ladies are not supporters of the Patriots, then?" he inquired, as the girls were herded towards their rooms to get ready for bed.

"Not us! They're a bunch of cheating cheaters who cheat!" replied Renee.

"If I saw Tom Brady, I would punch him in the knees! In the KNEES!" Lauren jabbed at the air to illustrate.

"I believe you, truly," said Brother Richard, amused. "And may I ask, which faction *do* you favor?"

"The Seahawks!" both girls chorused. Brother Kam and Brother Earl glanced at each other significantly, before turning their attention back to the girls. Brother Richard opened his mouth as if to speak again, but seemed to decide against it.

"That's enough, girls, stop bothering our guests. Off to bed with you, now. Shoo!" said their mother, guiding them towards their rooms. "Brothers, you'll find that the guest house out back has been made up for you. Please make yourselves comfortable, and we'll see you in the morning." The last the girls saw of the monks, they were rising from the table, stretching their stiff limbs, and making their way towards the back door.

It was late at night, the crickets still chirping, the first birds not yet stirring, when Lauren was awakened by a prod in the ribs from her sister. Renee held a finger to her lips, warning her to be silent. "There's a light on in the monks' cottage," she whispered into Lauren's ear. "They were looking at us so strangely after dinner, I'm sure they're up to something out there. Let's go check it out."

Lauren was always up for an adventure, so she rose, and throwing a coat on over her pajamas, followed her sister out the back door, stepping over their snoozing golden retriever.

Like silent shadows, the girls glided across the back yard towards the guest cottage. Against the far wall was a trellis, which, when climbed, led up to an easily opened attic window; it was in this attic that the girls often played when the cottage was empty. Boosting Lauren up first, Renee shinned up the wooden lattice and slipped inside. Moving slowly on their bellies, making not a single sound, they crawled to the trapdoor that led down into the main living area. Putting their eyes to the crack between the door and its jamb, this is what they saw.

There was indeed a light on in the living room of the cottage. The monks' brown robes lay flung over the arm of the largest couch, while the monks themselves were gathered around the coffee table, hunched forward in urgent conversation.

Without their robes, the brothers' appearance was much changed; they now wore snug-fitting tunics of shimmering fabric, the color of the midnight sky. Their chests and backs were adorned with decorations of blazing green and sparkling silver; on their feet were shoes of the same shades. Embroidered on each of their sleeves, stylized birds of prey scowled fiercely.

"Those aren't monks," breathed Renee. "Those are Seahawks."

Indeed, there was no mistaking the men in their resplendent uniforms; they could be nothing other than knights of the famed Seattle Seahawks. Brother Kam and Brother Earl were seated side by side on the couch, leaning over to consult a map spread over the coffee table. Brother Richard stood at the fireplace with his back to them, the fire illuminating his face with a golden glow.

"We could try Butte next," Brother Earl was saying, pointing at a spot on the map. "It's on the way to Bozeman. With the university there, perhaps we'd have better luck."

Brother Richard snorted. "Butte. I'm sure there are plenty of princesses in Butte, Montana. You can hardly throw a brick without hitting one, is what I hear." He stared moodily into the flames. "If only I knew what Pete was thinking when he sent us out to this godforsaken nowhere."

It was at this moment, inevitably, that up in the attic Renee leaned just a hair too far forward. The rusty latch of the trapdoor gave way, and in a cloud of plaster dust, both girls tumbled through space, landing on the coffee table and splintering it to matchsticks.

Dazed, Renee felt enormous hands lifting her up, dusting her off. When she could focus her vision again, she was sitting on the sofa, facing the fireplace. The three Seahawks were ranged in front of her, Brother Richard in the middle, flanked by Earl and Kam. "Are you unharmed, young lady?" asked Brother Richard.

Renee sputtered and spat plaster dust. "You're not monks! You're Seahawks! Why did you lie to us?"

The Seahawks looked at each other in silence. "Better tell her," said Brother Earl. "She may be able to tell us where to go next."

Brother Richard hesitated, then nodded, acquiescing. "Young lady, you are correct, we are Seahawks. I am called Sir Richard Sherman, and these are Sir Kam Chancellor and Sir Earl Thomas." He bowed slightly, dreadlocks cascading over his shoulders. "We are travelling the length and breadth of the land on an important quest for our leader, King Pete Carroll of Seattle. We disguised ourselves as monks so as not to be recognized on the road."

"If you don't want to be recognized, then maybe you shouldn't use your real names." Renee brushed plaster dust from her hair. "Just a thought."

Sir Earl elbowed Sir Kam. "Pete said that the first one would be wise."

"Quiet, Earl," said Sir Richard. He turned back to Renee. "Now, as I was saying, we travel the length and breadth of the land on an important que–ow!" He flinched and shrugged, trying to shake something off his back. He flailed, batting impotently over his shoulders. "Something's biting me! Kam, Earl, get it off!"

"Hold still, Richard. She's on there pretty good." Sir Kam grabbed something and pulled hard. A tiny figure came away from Sir Richard's back, growling and thrashing.

"Jesus. What is it?" said Sir Richard, rubbing the sore spot between his shoulders.

"That's my sister," said Renee.

"Yup, it's the little one, all right," Sir Kam confirmed, depositing her on the couch next to Renee. "Looks like she chewed her way right through your armor."

"Don't be mad," said Renee, fearing her sister would get in trouble. "It's nothing personal. She's a were-bearsnake, so she ambushes people every so often. It's just what she does."

"When you fell through the ceiling, I thought that was the attack signal, so I pounced," said Lauren, plucking shreds of Sir Richard's uniform out of her teeth. "Sorry."

Brother Earl raised his eyebrows. "The second one will be brave, Pete said."

"They're only children, Earl."

"Go ahead and ask them, Richard," interjected Sir Kam. "What can it hurt?'

Sir Richard considered this. "Very well," he said, finally, turning back to the girls. "Young ladies, I want you to think carefully. Has anyone ever told you, or have you ever heard, that you have royal blood in your veins?"

"Oh, of course," replied Renee promptly. "My grandpa was the king of France for about a day and a half, back in the seventies."

Sir Richard blinked. "Can it be true?" he said softly. "Can these children be the ones we seek?"

"Less musing, more explaining," ordered Renee. "You've kept us in the dark long enough."

Sir Richard looked back at Sir Kam and Sir Earl. Small nods from both. "All right, then. As I was saying, we have been sent by King Pete on a very important quest. The details I cannot tell you, not here, but you may know that we seek two princesses, the first very wise, and the second very brave. The very fate of the empire hangs in the balance." He let the unspoken question hang in the air.

"This quest," said Renee. "Is it like an adventure?"

"A great adventure. The first step would be to travel back to Seattle, to receive further instructions from King Pete."

"Well, this family just happens to be really good at adventures. I'm in," said Renee. "Lauren?"

"I go where you go," said Lauren loyally.

"Looks like you found your princesses. We'll get our bikes and meet you by the mailbox at first light." Renee jumped off the sofa and, taking Lauren by the hand, strolled out the door towards the big house, leaving the three dumbfounded Seahawks staring after them.

A delicate, shell-pink dawn was breaking over the Rockies as the three knights led their steeds down the path from the barn towards the mailbox. Renee and Lauren were already there, bikes leaning against the fence, stuffed packs upon their backs. Renee jumped down from the fencepost as Sir Richard waved a silent greeting. "We're ready. Where to?"

Sir Richard pointed west, towards the mountain passes still shrouded in gray gloom. "That way. Seattle."

"All right, then. After you." With a creaking of saddle leather and a soft squeaking of bicycle wheels, the party mounted up and set off down the road.

They were nearly out of town when Renee raised a hand. "Hold up here a minute."

"What's wrong?" Sir Richard reined his horse to a stop.

"Nothing, I just want to tell my uncle Joey where we're going. He's good at adventures; maybe he'll have some advice for us before we go." She pointed off into a field, where a light glimmered in the window of a hulking, tumbledown structure.

"All right," said Sir Richard. "But hurry. Time grows shorter every moment."

Renee hastened across the field and squeezed through the cracked door. Inside was a single large room, almost entirely filled with the gears, wheels and levers of a giant machine. Catwalks and ladders crawled over and across its many surfaces. A large hollow cylinder protruded at an angle near the top, pointed towards a roughly cut hole in the roof. From somewhere inside there came the sound of tinkering.

"Uncle Joey? Are you in here?" Renee squinted in the low light.

A hatch in the side of the machine creaked open, and out popped Uncle Joey's fuzzy head, a pair of heavy goggles perched above his eyebrows. "Renee! Hang on a second, I'll be right with you." The hatch clanged shut, footsteps clattered down an unseen ladder, and a moment later, Uncle Joey emerged from behind a tangle of iron piping. "What's shaking, squirt?"

"I just wanted to let you know that some knights came by our house last night. They need help with a quest, so Lauren and I are going to ride to Seattle with them today. Can you tell Mom I won't be home for dinner, or breakfast, or lunch for a little while?" Renee said this quickly, hoping that it didn't sound as ridiculous as it did.

Joey wiped his goggles with a greasy rag. "Sounds like an adventure. What kind of quest is it?"

Renee looked down. "They won't say. They told me that only King Pete Carroll can tell the whole story. I guess we'll find out when we get to Seattle."

"Following mysterious strangers on an unnamed quest with little to no idea of what lies ahead. I'm sure your mom won't be worried at all." Joey replaced the goggles on his head. "I'd go with you, but I'm kind of tied up here. Your Aunt

Laura is almost finished with her device to shoot the moon out of the sky, and she says she needs an extra pair of hands."

"Why does she want to shoot the moon out of the sky?"

"Oh, you know. She gets these ideas."

Renee nodded. She knew all about Aunt Laura's ideas. "Well, I guess we'd better get going. Do you have any advice for our first adventure?"

Uncle Joey considered. "Don't trust the gods. At least, not the Greek ones. Or the Norse. And watch out for the devil. That guy's an asshole."

"Um, OK." Renee shouldered her pack. "Is Bridger around at all? Maybe he'd have some, er, *other* advice." She caught herself before she said *better*.

"Nah, he's been off his tits on peyote all week. Could be another couple of days before he straightens out. But I'll tell him you said hi." Inside the machine, an engine began to thrum and gears began to clank. Joey sparked an acetylene torch. "Have fun on your adventure."

"We will! Bye!" Renee scurried to the door. She knew it was best to keep well clear of Aunt Laura's experiments.

Outside, the knights were patiently waiting. "All is well?" asked Sir Richard as Renee mounted her bike.

"Yep. Let's go." Renee led the way as they moved off down the road. Behind them, the machine in its house continued to hum and chug. The sound seemed to increase as they went, following them down the path. The thrum grew to a whine, and then a shriek. Suddenly, a beam of incandescent blue light shot out of the machine's barrel, through the hole in the roof, and lasered the top off nearby Lolo Peak.

"Damn it!" came Aunt Laura's voice from inside the house. "Reload! I think I know what we did wrong."

Sir Richard looked at Renee. "Just keep riding," she said.

High in his eyrie at the Palace of CenturyLink, King Pete Carroll gazed out over the leaden landscape. On the field below, the knights of the Seahawks ran halfhearted drills in the whistling wind. The Blue Thunder drum line tapped listlessly on the sidelines. *How much it has changed, and in such a short time*, Pete thought, resting his stately silver head on his hand. *Only two years ago, only two, the men would have been singing and shouting as they practiced, competing to see who could outdo the others in exuberance. Now, it is nothing but barren, joyless workmanship.*

Behind him, a door slid open. A handsome, leonine-featured young man entered. "Sir."

King Pete did not turn. "Russell. What news?"

"Sir Jimmy, Sir Thomas, and Sir Doug have returned. They arrived an hour ago."

"And?"

Lord Russell Wilson sighed. "Nothing."

King Pete closed his eyes. "Then it is all up to Sir Richard and his men. They are our last hope."

As if in answer, trumpets blared from the palace ramparts. King Pete's eyes snapped open as he jumped to his feet. On the field below, the men had abandoned their practice, leaving their equipment where it lay. Each man chattered to his neighbor, excitement spreading from helmet to helmet as they inclined their heads together. Some knights laughed aloud and clapped their hands, others danced jigs and slapped each other on the back. At the door, a page screeched to a halt, a folded paper clutched in white knuckles. "A message, sire!" he squeaked.

"What is it, Russell? What has happened?'

Lord Russell took the paper, unfolded it, and read. He sucked his breath in, looking up sharply. "Sir Richard and his party have returned. They have two princesses with them."

Below, the men were swarming around the tunnel that led to the field. The Blue Thunder drummers made the air pulse like a pumping heart, and the 12 flag flapped frenetically overhead. Finally, as the excitement reached fever pitch, Sir Richard, weary, travel-stained, and triumphant, emerged from the darkness, flanked by Sir Kam and Sir Earl. The men jubilated wildly, waving their arms and cheering.

Sir Richard held up a hand for quiet, and a reverent hush fell over the crowd. Some of the men knelt. From the darkness inside the tunnel came a faint squeaking, as of a chain needing oil. Finally, out of the gloom, there rode two small girls on pink bikes, carrying backpacks emblazoned with Moana and Spider-Man, respectively. The smaller girl's bike still had training wheels.

On the field, dead silence. In the eyrie, King Pete set his jaw. "Feed them. Bathe them. And assemble the Council."

"Sir." Lord Russell Wilson bowed, and departed.

Evening. The field of CenturyLink was deserted. The 12 flag hung motionless in the dead air. Then, through the gathering darkness came silent, hurrying figures, converging on the palace. In ones and twos, they glided up to the main door, spoke a few words, and entered. Inside, pages took their outer cloaks, revealing men in resplendent, multicolored finery, decorated with badges and sigils that proclaimed their origins. They greeted each other with nods but spoke little, following torch bearers through the winding passages of the palace until, one by one, they were shown into King Pete's eyrie.

The room was darkened, blinds drawn down over the floor-to-ceiling windows. In the center of the chamber stood a large, circular table, over which floated a hologram of a fearsome seahawk. As the room filled with guests of all different colors and sizes, it resembled that scene in every single Star Wars movie where the leaders of the alien races gather around a hologram of the Death Star.

The room filled. Pages circulated with snacks and drinks. As each new arrival entered, the assembled men scanned his face for clues. The question hung in the air, unasked but palpable. *What are we doing here?*

Finally, with his customary flourish, King Pete swept into the room, trailed by Lord Russell, Renee, and Lauren. Eyebrows raised and looks were exchanged as the guests noticed the girls, but nobody spoke aloud.

"Are we all here?" asked King Pete, turning to survey the group. "All thirty-one of us?" Nods and murmurs of assent. "Very well, then. Gentlemen, you know my quarterback, Lord Russell. And may I present as well my honored guests, Princess Renee and Princess Lauren, of Missoula, Montana."

"Hi." The girls waved.

"Pete, what is this?" burst out an elderly man clad in purple and gold. "You sent out the call not four hours ago, with no explanation, saying only *come at once*. What is going on? What news have you heard that requires us to come all this way on such short notice?"

King Pete bowed. "A worthy question, Baron Zimmer. You will have your answer, but first, I would like to review some background, to make sure that we are all aware of the situation as it now stands." Motioning the girls to take a seat beside the hologram table, he tapped a few buttons at the table's edge. The seahawk flickered and dissolved, replaced by flowing images of knights in motion.

"As some of you know, until recently, the Empire of the NFL was a happy, joyful place." Pete intoned. "Knights practiced, trained, and competed. Sometimes they won great battles. And when they won, they were free to celebrate openly, with their teammates, before the people of the community. These celebrations brought the people together, erased the differences between them, and sowed contentment over the land." Above the table, three hologrammatic knights high-stepped and high-fived before a backdrop of ecstatic onlookers. "It was an innocent time. A happy time. But it was not to last."

The hologram flickered again, changing to an image of a man who looked like a butternut squash in a suit. "The Emperor of the NFL, Roger Goodell, previously a benevolent ruler, suffered a spell of madness, in which he declared that celebrations were the source of much misery and unhappiness in the land. Forthwith, he banned their practice in public, except in such token ways as to be meaningless." The hologrammatic knights reappeared, sharing a tepid shoulder pat in an end zone. Behind them, the crowd yawned and texted. "Though he cannot prevent us from expressing ourselves here in our own palace, to celebrate where the people can see us has become a crime."

"A crying shame," someone in the assembly muttered. "Hear, hear," someone else put in.

"We all wondered what was the cause of the Emperor's sudden edict," King Pete continued. "Is he ill? Has his mind been poisoned against his own people? Finally, through a stroke of luck, the answer has come to us." The hologram shimmered once more, changing to an image of a squat, toadlike man dressed in a ratty sweatshirt, as tubby and slovenly as King Pete was dapper and trim. The assembly hissed. "Yes, of course, it is our old enemy, Duke Bill Belichick of Foxborough Hall. Information has come to me that he is responsible for blackmailing — yes, blackmailing! — the Emperor into issuing the excessive celebration rule, for his own nefarious reasons."

"And what reasons would those be, Pete?" Baron Mike Zimmer sounded skeptical.

"My source inside Foxborough Hall indicates that the strong feelings of joy which our celebrations elicit are interfering with the hypno drones that the Patriots of Foxborough use to maintain the loyalty of their people. Only those who are sedated by extreme smugness are susceptible, and for this reason, it benefits Duke Belichick to sabotage the happiness of others."

King Pete waved a hand, and the hologram of Belichick dissolved into an image of a moated fortress. "What is to be done, you are no doubt wondering. My source inside Foxborough does not dare reveal himself, not yet, but he has told me that the Duke keeps the blackmail material close at hand, on a thumb drive in his personal film review room, adjacent to his quarters." He wiped his brow, aware that this was where things were going to get weird. "This confidential source being unable to help us at this time, I was forced to look elsewhere for someone to infiltrate Foxborough and retrieve the drive. I wracked my brains, day after day, until finally, late one evening, I was visited by the spirit of Tony Romo. He told me to look for two princesses, one very wise and the other very brave, who would help us to recover the drive, restore the Emperor's peace of mind, and lift the excessive celebration rule. As soon as dawn broke, I sent my finest knights out to seek these princesses, wherever they might be." He held his hand out, presenting Renee and Lauren. "And now, after so much searching, here they are."

A cricket chirped outside. Finally, after a long silence, Baron Zimmer spoke. "Pete," he said gently, "did they not just legalize a whole bunch of drugs here in Washington?"

"I don't see what that has to do with anything." King Pete looked mortally offended.

"Well, for starters, Tony Romo isn't dead, so if his ghost is coming around telling you to kidnap little girls for some crazy quest, I have to assume that some pharmaceuticals were involved."

King Pete huffed. "I said I saw his spirit, not his ghost. All quarterbacks gain the ability to astrally project themselves when they retire, you know that." Shrugs and murmurs of reluctant agreement from the council.

"Even if we do believe you, Pete, these are just children. How can they possibly get past the Duke to retrieve the blackmail material?" This from a portly man wearing a blue satin jacket and a pedostache.

"We were all rookies once, Ben," returned King Pete. "It's not training that counts most, it's the talent."

A purse-lipped, bespectacled man in a turquoise polo shook his head. "I agree with McAdoo," he said. "The risk is too great. Even if what you say is true, we have to find another way."

"But, Ron–" There were growls and mutters from all directions. The mood in the room was turning. King Pete, his plan crumbling, looked helplessly around.

"*Everyone be quiet!*" Renee's voice cut through the hubbub. The men stopped talking and regarded the tiny, pink-clad girl in their midst.

"You know, this reminds me of the time that my Uncle Joey defeated the devil. The second time, not the first time. You see, my Aunt Laura got kidnapped by the Flathead Lake

Monster, so Uncle Joey dove to the bottom of the lake to find her, which turned out to lead into a cave. And that cave had a doorway that led into Hell, and through that doorway Uncle Joey could see footprints, so he followed them all the way to the devil's mansion. And the devil remembered Uncle Joey from the first time they met, and he said–"

"Little girl," said Baron Zimmer patiently, "what is the point of this story, if you please?"

"A diversion," replied Renee.

"A what?"

"Haaaaeeeeeee!" Lauren shot out from underneath the hologram table, darted across the floor like an arrow, and clamped her jaws onto Ben McAdoo's knee. He shrieked, caught off balance, and pitched to the floor. Growling deep in her throat, she gave him the dead roll, twisting her body to crack bone and cartilage. McAdoo flapped his hands, trying to fend her off, but it was no use, and in a moment, there was only the sound of Lauren crunching as she fed.

Renee looked at King Pete. "When do we leave for Foxborough?"

King Pete blinked. "Tomorrow. At dawn."

"Excellent," said Renee.

First light found the girls, King Pete, and Lord Russell back in the eyrie. The girls were kitted out in head-to-toe Patriots gear. "Lauren, I know it's ugly, but just try to deal with it," said Renee to her squirming sister, tugging distastefully at her own lumpy red-and-blue hoodie. "We'll need these disguises to get into Foxborough without being noticed."

"You have your map, yes? You remember your instructions?"

Renee patted her pocket. "Map is right here. We sneak into Foxborough with the rest of the crowds for the Duke's weekly feast. As usual, he will leave the feast early to prepare for the next week's battles. We follow him to the film room, create a diversion to lure him away, and grab the thumb drive while he's distracted. Then we hightail it back here, and we all go to the Emperor to tell him to lift the excessive celebration rule."

"Very good. This will be your transport to Foxborough." Lord Russell opened the small box he carried, and from it King Pete withdrew a small, glittering object. "Here. Be very careful. It is the only one." He stooped to hand it to her.

Renee took the object, a weighty golden ring encrusted with jewels. "Your Super Bowl ring."

"Indeed." King Pete nodded gravely. "It is very precious. In order to use it, hold it tightly in your hand until it heats up, and say the name of the place you wish to go. It will transport you there instantly. But mind you don't lose it, for if you do, you will be stranded at Foxborough Hall, and we will have no way to help you." He straightened up. "Now then, are you both ready?"

Renee looked at Lauren. "Yes, we are."

"Very good. Our spy at Foxborough has promised to lower the power on the hypno drones today, so they should not affect you. Nevertheless, you must hurry, and come back to us before they return to full power at midnight."

"Got it." Renee took a deep breath and her sister's hand. She clutched the ring tightly in her fingers. As Pete had warned, it first grew warm, then burning hot. "FOXBOROUGH HALL!" she cried.

Traveling by Super Bowl ring is like flying through a storm of blue fire. Iridescent sparks flew from Renee and Lauren's bodies as they rushed onward through the swirling void, as if caught in a river's current. As they traveled, they shot past black holes in the storm, portals to other destinations. Finally, through an opening dead ahead, they hurtled back into normal space, landing on a pile of hay in a corner of the main courtyard of Foxborough Hall.

Renee was the first to regain her senses. Slowly she sat up, brushing alfalfa from her hair, and looked around. The courtyard was so crowded with people that no one seemed to have noticed their arrival. Like a migrating herd of bison, they streamed over the drawbridge lowered across the moat, heading for a hulking, stone-faced building with doors standing open. Outside, through the gateway, Renee could see the blood-red skies of Massachusetts, glowing grimly over the blackened, twisted landscape.

"Moo." A wet-nosed ox nudged Renee, urging her to get out of his dinner. By now, Lauren was stirring as well.

Renee helped her sister to her feet. "Come on. I bet if we follow the crowd, we'll find out where the Duke is." She tucked the Super Bowl ring securely in her pocket, and shaking dirt, hay, and a last few blue sparks from their clothes, they joined the slow-moving herd, letting it sweep them through the doors and into the Great Hall of Foxborough.

Inside the great hall, torches blazed. Rows of trestle tables filled the space, groaning under the weight of the lavish banquet laid out upon them. At the far end of the room, opposite a roaring fireplace, stood a high table on a dais, behind which a row of nobles sat.

Renee recognized the Hutt-esque figure in the center, at the place of honor. She nudged Lauren. "Look, there, that's Duke Belichick. And the guy next to him must be the prince, Tom Brady." She indicated by a nod a blandly attractive, Ken doll-type young man, slouched in an upholstered chair, attention buried in a chirping Game Boy.

"Let's try to get closer." Taking her sister's hand, Renee began threading her way through the crowd towards the high table. Lauren grabbed a turkey leg off a passing tray with her free hand and began to gnaw as they worked their way along. "Don't eat too much, Lauren. We need you hungry for this job."

"Just a little snack–" Lauren's reply was cut short by the booming voice of Duke Belichick, who had risen behind the high table, and was addressing the crowd with an upraised goblet.

"Loyal friends, I thank you for joining us on this auspicious evening!" the duke proclaimed. "You have the sincere appreciation of myself and Prince Tommy here– Tommy, can you put that down for a minute?" He pointed at the Game Boy.

"Tuh!" Tom Brady rolled his eyes and cracked the wad of gum he was chewing, but he paused his game and set it on the edge of the table. Still slouched in his seat, he scuffed the toes of his sneakers in the sawdust on the floor.

"Thank you, sweetheart." Duke Belichick turned back to the crowd. "As I was saying, you have our sincere appreciation for your support during the last season of battles. As you know, not all knights are as, ahem, *fortunate* as ours, and I have heard reports of the discontent of other, lesser nobles, who envy our successes." The guests exchanged smirks and smug high-fives. The duke held up his hand, shaking his head in mock dismay. "Indeed, the jealousy of the inferior is sad, and it is small wonder that the supporters of these other knights now abandon them, and rally to our cause. But now, dear guests, eat and drink as much as you like, for there is room for all on the bandwagon of the Patriots!" Toasting the crowd with his goblet, the duke resumed his seat. Self-satisfied chants of *They hate us 'cause they ain't us!* reverberated around the hall as the guests fell to feasting. By now, Renee and Lauren had crept close enough to the high table to hear the duke's conversation.

"Daddy, can I go to the mall with Stacey a little later?" Prince Brady had recovered his Game Boy and was tapping away at the controls. "She says that they're releasing a new smoothie flavor at the Jamba Juice, and all the popular knights are going to be there."

"Well, I don't know about that, darling. You remember we agreed, no hanging out at the mall with Stacey until you finish your film review for the week."

Brady pouted. "You are *ruining* my life. Absolutely *everyone* is going to be there to taste the new smoothie, and I'm going to be the *only* one who misses it, and nobody will *ever* invite me anywhere again!" He blew and popped a few sulky bubbles, then continued in a more wheedling tone. "I promise I'll be back in plenty of time for film review. Gronk can drive us in the hover jet."

"No can do." This was from a broad-shouldered, crop-headed young man on Duke Belichick's right, working intently on a laptop. "The hypno drones have been operating at half power all day, and the only way to fix it is to go through the code line by line. If I can't get them back to full strength soon, we may see our hold on the countryside slipping."

Duke Belichick turned back to the prince, shrugging helplessly. "Sweetheart, you know the hypno drones are very important to our plans. If Gronk needs to work on them, don't you think that's just a little more important than giving you and Stacey a ride to the mall?"

'Oh, sure, whatever Gronk wants. It's always all about whatever Gronk wants," Prince Brady huffed. "Nobody cares about me. Nobody would care if I just disappeared!" Shoving his Game Boy into his back pocket, he jumped to his feet and stomped off, exiting through an archway and running, half in tears, up a stone staircase.

Duke Belichick sighed. "I'm going to go get started on film review while he cools down, and then I'll go talk to him. Gronk, you keep working on the drones, and come let me know when they're operational again." Gronk, not looking up from his laptop, gave a thumbs up. Looking out over the feast a final time, the duke sighed once more, and departed up the stairs.

"Now's our chance," whispered Renee to Lauren. "If we can spy on him in the film review room, maybe he'll give away the hiding place of the thumb drive. Let's go." Ducking low, they dodged past a couple of guards, momentarily distracted by a drunken reveler, and darted up the stairs after the duke.

Up the spiral staircase and through winding, torch-lit corridors the girls tiptoed, following the echoing footsteps of the duke. Finally, they heard the footsteps pause, a door being opened, and the creak of a leather chair. A drawer slid open and shut, a computer chimed awake, and a keyboard clicked. The girls crept forward and peeked through the crack of the door.

Through the gap, the girls looked into a spacious, well-appointed chamber. The red and blue carpet was thick enough to lose a hamster in, gilt-framed mirrors and portraits lined the walls, and the furniture was richly upholstered in silk and hides. By the window was a simple wooden desk, at which the duke sat with his back to the door, typing a password into his computer. As it booted up, he fished in the top drawer, extracting a thumb drive, which he plugged into the USB slot. Renee elbowed Lauren. "There it is!" she whispered.

But as the drive opened and the duke selected files, they were disappointed, for the computer showed only video of knights in Patriots uniforms, at practice and in battle. The duke frowned, evidently displeased by something in the video, and withdrawing a pad and pen from the desk, began to scribble notes. Beside her, Renee felt the familiar tensing of Lauren about to charge. She put a restraining hand on her sister's shoulder. "Not yet," she whispered into Lauren's ear. "Just wait. He may show us where the blackmail drive is."

Footsteps sounded, and a door on the opposite side of the room swung open, admitting Prince Tom Brady, his eyes red and puffy. "Daddy?" he sniffled theatrically. "Stacey just called. Did you decide if I could go to the mall with her?" He jutted his lower lip, making it tremble with the threat of another tantrum.

The duke looked up from his computer, hesitated. "Will you promise to do your film review as soon as you get home afterwards?"

"I promise. I'll even do an extra hour, to get a jump on next practice."

The duke sighed. "Very well. You may go to the mall with Stacey."

"Hooray!" The prince danced a few steps, clapping his hands, the threat of tears evaporated. "Thank you, Daddy! I love you!" He stopped a moment. "Is Gronk going to take us in the hover jet, then, or will you give us a ride?"

"No, Gronk is busy. I'll do it." The duke heaved himself out of his chair. "Wait here while I get my coat. Won't be a minute." He paused at the far door. "Remember, extra film review before bedtime."

"It's as good as done." The prince was already at one of the mirrors, checking the artful feathering of his hair. Duke

Belichick sighed again and departed, his footsteps receding beyond the door.

The prince hummed to himself as he arranged his clothes and hair in the mirror. "Who's a pretty fella? You are! Who, me? Yes, you are!" He winked at his reflection, adjusting his shirt just so over his biceps, but as he took his hand away, the fabric wrinkled and puckered. The prince frowned. "Hmmm. Might have put a little too much in last time. Better fix it before Stacey sees." Opening the drawer of a side table, he pulled out a small bicycle pump and inserted the needle under the skin of his arm. So intent was he that he did not notice a shadow passing across the light of the chandelier overhead. He pulled back on the pump's plunger, withdrawing air, then repeated the process on the other arm. Pulling out the needle, he flexed in the mirror again. The shirt now fit perfectly. "That's better." The prince smiled at himself, self-satisfied.

"*Heeeeeeeeaaaaaaa!*" Lauren dropped from the chandelier onto the prince's shoulders, dragging him backward.

"*Guuuuuuugggggggllhhh!*" The prince tried to cry out, but was silenced by Lauren's arm locked around his throat. He thrashed and flailed wildly, knocking over furniture and decorations, trying to dislodge the tiny demon from his back. As he struck at her, the sleeve of his shirt slipped up, and Lauren sank her sharp little teeth into his bicep.

Sssssssssssssssss. The sound of escaping air made the prince's eyes widen in terror. Panicking, he tried to crush Lauren against the stone wall of the chamber, but the pressure only accelerated the leak, and as she tightened her grip, she could feel his body growing limp and squishy. The skin of his face sagged, eyes showing their whites. He staggered, his legs buckling under her weight, and then collapsed, the last air slowly wheezing out of the hole in his arm. He was still. Lauren growled and took cover under a divan, dragging after her the deflated remains of Prince Tom Brady.

"Good job, Lauren!" Renee was already at the computer, opening and closing files on the thumb drive. "Not this one. Or this one. Maybe there's another drive." She jerked open the top drawer. "Oh, hell."

The drawer was filled with identical thumb drives, hundreds of them, each labeled only with a date. *Of course, it makes perfect sense,* thought Renee. *He would hide it in plain sight. Nobody would ever go through all these old film review files, so no one would ever stumble on the blackmail file by chance.*

There was no time to go through them all. She rifled through the drives, looking for any clue that might point her in the right direction.

By sheer chance, the eighth drive she looked at caught her eye. The date said 32/13/69. Renee frowned. King Pete had described Duke Belichick as slobby in appearance but meticulous in practice, so why would he label a drive with a day and month that did not exist? Furthermore, he could not possibly have been leading the Patriots in 1969, for that was years before the glaciers had receded from Massachusetts, and the area would have still been ruled by woolly mammoths and dire wolves. She plugged in the drive. It contained one file, rubberducky.mov. She clicked it.

On the screen, the image wobbled, then stabilized. It appeared to be from a hidden camera in a bedroom, covering a dresser with a stereo on top, a blue shag rug, and a full-length mirror in a corner. For several seconds, nothing happened.

Then a man stepped in from the left side of the frame. It was the same sandy-haired man that Renee had seen in King Pete's hologram. He was wearing a bright yellow latex suit that covered him from throat to toes, and as he took up his position in front of the mirror, he pulled a matching yellow mask over his head. As he turned to push a button on the stereo, Renee saw that the mask featured painted, bugged-out eyes and an upturned orange bill over the man's mouth. "Dear God," she breathed.

On the monitor, the man snapped his fingers, counting out a measure for nothing. Then, as jazzy music poured from the stereo, he began to sashay and strut before the mirror. *"Rubber ducky, you're the one,"* he sang in a cracking voice. *"You make bath time so much fun."* He picked up a brimming glass from just out of frame and tipped sudsy water over his own head. The yellow latex undulated hypnotically.

Renee had seen enough. She clicked the file closed, jerked the drive free, and pocketed it. "Got it! Lauren, let's g–"

"A-HA!" A hand on the collar of her hoodie lifted Renee out of her seat. The duke shook her, hard. "I should have known that Pete would send his minions, but I didn't expect that he would send girls!" Renee scratched and kicked. "Well, we know what to do with spies here at Foxborough. TOMMY! GET IN HERE!" he roared. He stuck his hand into the pocket of her hoodie, grabbing what was inside.

Prying at his fingers, Renee managed to twist free, dropping to the ground. "Tommy's not coming!" she taunted, trying to distract him. "And I know what you've been doing to the Emperor, and I'm gonna tell!"

Fist still clenched around his prize, he hurled a book at her, and she dodged. "What have you done to Tommy, you brat?"

"Tommy's the brat!" she yelled back. "If you didn't spoil him so much, maybe he'd have been better behaved!" *Just a few more seconds*, she thought.

"Where is he?" the duke screamed. Renee jerked her chin at the shadow under the divan, where a flattened, deflated foot protruded. The duke howled. "I'LL KILL YOU!" As he started for Renee again, he suddenly registered that his fist was on fire.

The object he had grabbed from Renee's pocket was burning hot, searing his palm. Instinctively, he parted his fingers to see what was hurting him. Gold flashed and diamonds glinted, as King Pete's Super Bowl ring reached its maximum power.

"THE BERKELEY PIT!" screamed Renee.

Blue fire. Snapping sparks. Rushing, rushing, breathless through the storm, until, dead ahead, a black hole opened in front of the duke. Then falling, falling through endless open air, a flat black surface hurrying upward to smack him in the face. A splash. And then, nothing.

Near Butte, Montana, on the shore of the Berkeley Pit, the most toxic and contaminated body of water in North America, two EPA employees in hazmat suits were raking poisonous glop into piles.

"Did you see that?" said one to the other.

"See what?"

"Some fat old guy just fell out of the sky screaming. He fell into the middle of the pit."

"And?" The second man continued raking.

"Well, should we tell someone? A supervisor, maybe?"

The second man stopped and leaned on his rake. "Look, Eddie, all's I know is, our job is to rake this glop. We don't get to go home until it's done, and if we stop to investigate every fat guy who falls out of the sky into the pit, we are going to be here all god damn day. So let's get back to work." He bent and resumed raking. After a long pause, Eddie shrugged and did the same.

Lauren helped Renee to her feet. "That was close," gasped Renee. "Lucky I remembered my Montana geography."

"Renee, the ring." Lauren's brow furrowed with concern.

"I know, I know. I lost it. We're going to have to find another way home." She took her sister by the hand, leading her towards the door they had come through. "Let's try going back the way we came."

"Duke Belichick? Is everything all right? I heard shouting." As the door swung open, the girls froze, for there on the other side stood the broad-shouldered, crop-headed young man from the banquet hall. His soft brown eyes took in the huddled girls, the scorch marks on the carpet caused by the duke's departure, and the deflated leg of Tom Brady sticking out from under the divan. Abruptly, he turned, beckoning them down the corridor. "Follow me. We don't have much time."

They had to trot to keep up with his long strides as he led them through the twisting halls. Finally, climbing up a final staircase, they emerged onto a wide, flat area atop one of the battlements, where a small hover jet waited. Beeping a remote, the young man opened the doors, handing Renee into the front passenger seat and Lauren into the back. "Here we go. It's a bit cramped, but you're small, so we should fit just fine."

He climbed up into the driver's seat, where the controls illuminated at his touch. "Seat belts, ladies." The engines whooshed as the young man guided the jet up and over the ramparts of Foxborough. "And away we go." The jet wheeled and sped off, towards the setting sun.

It was several minutes before Renee broke the silence. "So, thanks for the ride, Mister, erm, Gronk?"

"Sir Robert, actually. Robert Gronkowski, at your service." He held out his hand.

"Pleased to meet you." Renee took his hand and shook. "And like I was saying, thanks for the ride."

"My pleasure. I thought we'd head straight to New York, to save time, if it's all the same to you."

"I guess. What's in New York?"

"Emperor Goodell's house. The sooner he gets that drive, the better."

Realization dawned on Renee. "You're King Pete's sleeper at Foxborough."

Sir Robert smiled in the glow of the control console. "Pete said you were clever."

Renee grinned back. "So, it's New York, then?"

"Correct. We're already almost there." Sir Robert pointed to the wash of light on the horizon. "I'll just hit our cloaking device, so we don't freak anyone out when we land." He flipped a switch, and in the darkness outside, the hover jet shimmered and vanished. Inside, Sir Robert punched another button, flooding the cabin with music. "Landing tunes," he said cheerily.

He braked the hover jet over a lavish mansion in the suburbs, finessing the controls to set it down gently on the front lawn. The gull-wing door hissed open, and a silver gangway extended down to the ground. "Here we are, ladies. This is your stop."

"You're not coming with us?" Renee frowned. "The duke isn't coming back, and the prince is dead. You don't have to stay there anymore."

"Unfortunately, I do," replied Sir Robert. "I helped build the fleet of hypno drones that keeps the Patriots' army docile, and if they suddenly go offline, there's no telling what kind of mayhem could occur." He slid his fingers over the controls, reconfiguring the jet for takeoff. "I need to go back so I can begin to shut them down gradually. Perhaps I can steer the duchy in a better direction after this. It could be the dawning of a new era." He smiled at his own grandiosity. "Or something. Anyway, you should go now. The mission is in your hands."

Lauren was already out the door and on the lawn. Renee hesitated, then unbuckled her seatbelt. "All right. Thank you so much for everything. We won't forget you." She slid out of her seat and down the gangway.

"Nor I you, princesses." As the door glided shut, Sir Robert lifted a hand in farewell. "Good luck go with you." The warm backdraft of the jet's liftoff blew the girls' hair back, as they watched it rise, shimmer, and blink out of sight.

Renee took Lauren's hand and started towards the house. "Almost done."

Emperor Roger Goodell bubbled up from the depths of sleep, blearily aware that it was far too early to be awake. No birds sang, no crickets chirped, and the sky outside his window was pitch black. He rolled over to check his alarm clock. 2:17 a.m. "'Shit," he said.

"That's a naughty word." The emperor yelped, startled, and sat straight up in bed. He pressed back against the wall, cringing away from the two girls seated on the foot of his bed. "If our mom was here, she'd wash your mouth out with soap," said the bigger one.

"And then you'd be grounded. For a week at least," the smaller one added.

The emperor covered his eyes with his hands. "Okay, Roger, get a grip. This is only a dream. You had too much pie last night. There are not two small, scary girls in your bedroom. You just need to calm down, drink some water, and go back to sleep." He peeked through his fingers. The girls were still there. "God damn it."

"Quiet. We're here on imperial business." Renee noted with some revulsion that the Emperor's blue flannel pajamas were printed with bright yellow duckies. "It's about Duke Belichick."

"Did Belichick send you? He's already got what he wants! I did exactly as he asked; I kept the knights from celebrating in public, even though the empire hates me for it. What more can I do than I've already done?" the emperor whined.

"Belichick is dead. So is Tom Brady." Renee cut him off. "We come with a message from King Pete Carroll." She slipped the thumb drive out of her pocket and held it out to him. "The message is: *don't fear the rubber ducky.*"

The emperor grabbed at the drive. "This is it? Are you sure?"

"I am. I wish I wasn't, but I am."

"Oh, thank Jesus." The emperor exhaled shakily. "It's over. It's finally over."

"Well, almost. You have one more thing to do, Emperor Goodell."

The emperor blinked in the moonlight. "What's that?"

"And therefore, effective immediately, the excessive celebration rule is repealed!" announced the emperor, standing behind a podium emblazoned with the imperial crest. Cameras flashed and tape recorders whirred. "Are there any questions? Yes, madam, you." He pointed at a reporter with her hand up.

She stood. "Emperor, it was less than two years ago that you banned excessive celebrations, saying that they were a corrupting influence on the people and detracted from the purity of the knights' battles. What caused you to change your mind?"

"I had an earnest discussion with some of the younger fans, and they persuaded me that, far from being detrimental, public displays of joy are essential for bringing the people together and fostering a sense of community. It definitely wasn't because I was being blackmailed. Next question." At the back of the room, Renee rolled her eyes.

Another reporter stood. "Sir, has there been any progress in the investigation into the disappearances of Duke Belichick and Prince Brady? I understand that neither of them has been heard from for several days."

"The investigation is ongoing," the emperor replied. "The only thing I can say for sure is that it is not being neglected in order to cover up foul play." Lauren facepalmed. More reporters waved hands or scribbled on pads; some rushed off to file their articles before the others.

Renee patted Lauren on the shoulder and nodded toward the exit. "Come on, let's get out of here before he gets into more hot water. We've done our part."

"Yeah. Plus we probably have school or something."

They walked out the front doors to the lawn, where the imperial helicopter waited to whisk them home. A liveried pilot helped them to their seats and strapped them in. As the rotors began to churn and the helicopter lifted off, Renee leaned over to her little sister's ear. "That was a good adventure, but I'm sure glad it's over!" she shouted.

"Me too!" Lauren agreed. The helicopter turned and began its uneventful flight towards Montana.

Moonlight shone on the barren shore of the Berkeley Pit. All was complete stillness, for everything that had ever lived in or near the Pit was dead. Piles of toxic glop lay on the banks, waiting to be raked the next day.

From the depths of the greenish black water rose a single oily bubble. It lingered on the surface for a long second, then popped, greasily, spreading slow ripples. Another bubble rose. Then two more. Beneath the turbid water, a shadow wavered and twisted–

With an oleaginous splash, a boiled, fleshless hand reached up from the Pit, clawing towards the crescent moon.

THE END?

How Joe, Bridger, Laura, Renee, and Lauren Saved the World from the Patriots, Again

The ragged, bearded man half-staggered, half-ran down the passageway, his rasping breaths echoing off the damp stone walls. His torn, filthy clothes hung from his long, scrawny limbs. He was tall, and looked as though he had once been a big, solid man, but now he was nearly emaciated.

With a breathless sob, he burst through the wooden door at the end of the corridor and stumbled towards the bank of computers arrayed against the far wall. Half-falling against the control console, he slapped at a glowing power button.

"Name?" said a bland computerized voice.

"Sir Robert Gronkoswki."

"Please present biometric verification." A glowing red oval flickered. The man pressed the pad of his index finger onto it, the nail broken and dirty. "Welcome, Sir Robert. What would you like to do today?" intoned the voice.

"Compose message." A blank screen flashed up, cursor blinking. The man rasped out a few words.

Behind him, the door slowly creaked open. "My, my," said a hoarse, whispery voice in the darkness. "What have we here? Our friend Gronk, out after curfew." A figure glided out of the shadows, its face obscured by a black hood. From the sleeves of its robe hung grey, twisted hands, the skin bubbled and melted.

The ragged man whirled and stared. "Send message," he croaked.

"I didn't understand. Please repeat." said the computer.

In the shadow of the hood, the robed figure smiled. "Now that is precious. Big, strong Gronk is trying to call for help."

"Send message." Eyes wide, the ragged man could barely manage a whisper.

"I didn't understand. Please repeat."

The robed one chuckled. "Are you there, Tommy? Are you seeing this?" he called over his shoulder.

"Yes, Father." A second figure stepped out of the gloom, a tallish man, standing ramrod straight. His short brown hair was precisely clipped and neatly combed. No lines marked his marble-smooth skin, and if he had ever smiled, it had left no traces on his perfect, Ken-doll face. His eyes were ice-blue and empty.

The robed one turned back to face the ragged man. "You really think you can get a message to anyone who can help you?" he growled. "You really think we haven't taken precautions? Are we the type of people who leave things to chance, Tommy?"

"No, Father." Tommy's face was emotionless.

"No, we aren't. We think of everything. That's why we are who we are." He clapped his gnarled hands together. "Well! High time that we were all in bed, I think. Tommy, do you have your zappers set to stun?"

220

"Yes, Father." Tommy's eyes began to glow, faintly at first, then increasing in brightness.

"Good boy. Now, get him!"

The ragged man shrank back against the console. "Send message!" he screamed. "Send message! Send message!"

Tommy's eyes blazed blue fire. With a shriek of burning ozone, twin rays of blinding light flashed out. The ragged man crumpled to the floor.

The computer's voice piped up. "Message sent."

It was another beautiful morning in Missoula. Renee and Lauren were seated at the high table in the breakfast nook, munching their cereal and watching the robins play on the lawn outside the window.

"Morning, squirts." Uncle Joe pushed open the front door and entered the house, followed by Aunt Laura. "How's it hanging?" He ruffled Lauren's hair as he passed toward the kitchen to greet the girls' mother.

"It's OK. We have to go to school soon." Renee jumped down and carried her cereal bowl to the sink to rinse, because she was a good girl who never left messes for her mother to clean up.

"Hey, that's cool. Are we still on to go to the carousel after that?"

"Carousel!" hollered Lauren, waving her spoon aloft like a sword.

"Yes, carousel. *After* school," said the girls' mother, wiping her hands on a towel. "Oh, I almost forgot. A message came in on the computer, addressed to you girls. I printed it out for you last night." She plucked a folded sheet of paper from the counter and passed it to Renee. Lauren, Joe, and Laura crowded around to read it.

"BELICHICK IS BACK." it read. "BRADY REVIVED. PLEASE HELP. ALL IS LOST WITHOUT YOU." Renee and Lauren looked at each other, nodded, and with one accord slid off their chairs, marching into their respective bedrooms.

"Belichick back?" Laura wondered aloud. "Isn't that the NFL coach who went missing last year?" Thumping and rattling came from inside the girls' rooms, along with the sound of zippers and snaps.

"Tom Brady, too," said Joe. "Vanished about the same time, and nobody's heard from him since."

The girls' bedroom doors banged open and they emerged, grim-faced, and made for the front door. They were armored like tanks in dirt bike pads, soccer shin guards, and bicycle helmets, with bulging packs on their backs. Renee carried a baseball bat, Lauren had a small sword left over from a Halloween costume.

"Just where do you two think you're going?" The girls' mother intercepted them at the welcome mat.

"You read the message," said Renee. "That was from Sir Robert Gronkowski, letting us know that Bill Belichick and Tom Brady have somehow survived. We have to go put them down, for good this time."

"And why you? What do Bill Belichick and Tom Brady have to do with two little girls in Missoula?"

Renee sighed. "You remember when Roger Goodell lifted the excessive celebration rule a year ago? That was because Lauren and I traveled to Foxborough Hall and defeated Brady and Belichick on their own ground, lifting their blackmail campaign against ol' Roger."

Their mother's eyes narrowed. "Uncle Joey said you were on a field trip."

"We didn't want you to worry," said Joe

"And now, if you'll excuse us–" Renee started to lead the way out the door. Their mother shifted to block their path.

"Absolutely not. You have school."

"But *Mom*." Renee whined. "The fate of humanity may hang in the balance. What if Belichick deploys his hypno-drones across the globe? We'll all be turned into Patriots fans!"

"Don't be ridiculous," said the girls' mother. "You're far too sensible to become a Patriots fan. Now take off all of that ridiculous gear, get your books back in your backpacks where they belong, and get ready for school, or there will be no carousel tonight."

Renee held her mother's stare for a long moment, then sagged in surrender. "Fine. But don't blame me if you suddenly start talking with a Boston accent."

Recess. Lauren had acquired a pointed stick and was working on digging a pretty good hole in the ground by the schoolyard fence, when she felt a tap on her arm. Looking up, she saw her sister, holding both of their backpacks and looking over her shoulder. "Lauren, we have to get out of here and get to Foxborough. Sir Robert is counting on us, and nobody else is going to do anything. We have to destroy Brady and Belichick, once and for all."

Lauren stood up, dusting off her jeans. "You had me at destroy," she said.

Renee squeezed her shoulder with sisterly affection. "I knew I could count on you." They looped the straps of their packs onto their shoulders, and, taking advantage of a playground teacher distracted by a fight, hopped the chain link fence and trotted towards home to retrieve their bikes.

It was a long way, so once they were out of sight of the school, they slowed to a walk. "We got to Foxborough by teleport last time," said Renee, "so I don't know how long it will take to ride there on our bikes. I only hope we're not too late."

"What's that I hear?" said a strange, dry voice. "Two little girls need to get somewhere in a hurry?" The girls stopped and looked around.

"Perhaps I can be of assistance, young ladies." The voice belonged to a tall, pale, cadaverous man of indeterminate age, leaning against a brick wall next to an alley. He was uncommonly well-dressed for Missoula, in black wool topcoat, pearl grey morning suit, and gleaming black patent leather shoes. A well-brushed black hat dangled from the fingers of his left hand, and a ruby stick pin sparkled in the perfect knot of his striped cravat. His close-lipped smile reminded Renee of a cat watching a soon-to-be-eaten goldfish.

"Going a long ways, are you?" the stranger continued in his cultured drawl. "Perhaps I can interest you in the very latest in bicycle technology." He snapped his fingers, and an unseen light illuminated the alley, revealing a pair of shiny pink ten-speeds, complete with saddlebags, bells, and streamers from the handlebars.

"How did you do that?" With one arm, Renee pressed Lauren back behind her. She wasn't sure what to make of the stranger, but his manner, together with his faint aroma of dead flowers, was making her nervous.

"Or perhaps the young ladies don't care to tire their legs by pedaling for such a long journey." The stranger clicked his fingers again. The light in the alley flickered, and the bicycles were replaced by a pair of sleek dirt bikes, engines already purring. "All gassed up and ready for the road. I have the contract all ready here. Reasonable terms." The stranger straightened and took a step toward the girls.

Renee stepped back, pressing Lauren behind her. "No, thanks, mister. No sale. C'mon, Lauren, we're late." She grabbed her sister's hand and pulled her down the sidewalk, not quite running, but walking briskly enough to put some distance between them and the stranger.

"Oh, girls?" called another voice, this one lower and gruffer. Looking up, the girls saw a wiry old man in the mouth of another alley, dressed only in a pair of ragged overalls and a straw hat. At his side stood a gigantic black dog, watching the girls intently. "Would you like to pet this nice doggie? He's very friendly, and he loves little girls. Don't you, Shukir?" The dog wagged once, never taking its eyes off the girls.

"Buzz off, creep," Renee muttered, giving the old man a wide berth as she and Lauren slipped past.

"Wait!" called the old man. "I have—"

"Oh, for fuck's sake, guys," boomed a third voice, deep as rolling thunder. "They're children. This is not hard." Renee pulled up to avoid running into the figure that stepped in front of her, blocking the sidewalk. She stared at the enormous, thickset man, nearly as broad as he was tall, regarding her from underneath a mop of glossy black ringlets. He grinned inside his luxuriant beard. "Time to go, girls."

"Listen mister, I don't know who you are, but I told you and your creepy friends to get lost!" Renee balled up her fists, and Lauren bared her tiny teeth."

"The name is Zeus. And I wasn't asking." The man laughed heartily, as sparks of electricity began to writhe through his beard. His eyes flashed and lightning crackled at his fingertips. Too late, the girls turned to run. White bolts shot from Zeus' hands, and they fell senseless to the ground.

The other two strangers ambled up the pavement. "Well, done, Zeus," observed the first one, the thin gentleman with the bicycles. "That can't have been heard by more than a hundred people."

Zeus grunted. "Listen, devil, just for that, you and Odin can carry them all the way to Foxborough yourselves. I did the heavy lifting."

The devil looked at old man Odin, who shrugged. Each of them scooped up a girl, slinging them over their shoulders. Odin reached behind a tree, pulling out a shining golden spear. "Stand close together, now," he said. 'Next stop, Foxborough

Hall." He began to twirl the spear point through the air, weaving a net of gold around the three men, the two girls and the dog. Faster and faster the spear whirled, until the figures were scarcely visible. Then the air shimmered, and they were gone.

"Where can they be?" Worriedly, the girl's mother checked the clock again. "I told them to be home by 3:00 sharp so we could go to the carousel." It was 4:01 pm. "I'm going to call some of their friends' houses." She disappeared into another room.

"What are you doing?" Laura leaned over to Joe, who was tapping at his phone.

"Texting Bridger. I have a weird feeling about this, and I think we may need backup."

Bridger must have been nearby, for before the girls' mother returned from the next room, there he was, knocking on the front door. "Hey, dude and dudette. What's going on?" said Bridger by way of greeting.

"Renee and Lauren haven't come back from school. We're worried."

"No shit, you're worried. You want to hop in the car and drive around to look for them?"

"Well, I'm not sure they're within easy driving distance." Bridger looked quizzical. "This morning before they left, they got a crazy message from someone called Sir Robert Gronkowski," Joe explained. "It said that Bill Belichick and Tom Brady are alive, and that only the girls can stop them from…something. The message ended there, but I think the girls ditched school and headed for Foxborough Hall to investigate."

Bridger whistled low. "Their mom is going to be *pissed* when she finds out."

"Exactly. So we need to get to them before she does. Are you up for a drive to Massachusetts?"

"Into the devil's den, eh?" Bridger took a swig from the flask that was his constant companion. "Sounds like an adventure. I'll go shovel the beer cans out of the car."

"I'll help you." said Joe. "We need to leave as soon as possible."

"You guys go ahead." said Laura, heading for the back door. "I need to get a couple things for the trip."

"Hurry!" Joe called after her retreating back. He pulled open the front door, and nearly collided with Grandpa Dave, who was just coming inside. "Dad! Are you here to help?" Grandpa Dave, children, is unpredictable at times, as you know, but there could be no denying that they needed all the aid they could muster.

"I just got the call from your sister." Dave said, stepping into the living room. "Just tell me what I can do."

"That's great, Dad. I was just telling Bridger that I think— wait, what are you wearing?"

"This?" said Dave, smoothing his shirt over his belly. "It's a Patriots jersey. Number 12, just like Tom Brady."

"Since when are you a Patriots fan?"

"Since when are you not? You can't argue with five Super Bowl rings." Dave scoffed. "You're not turning into one of those bandwagon Patriots haters, are you? They hate us 'cause they ain't us, you know."

Joe and Bridger exchanged a look that meant *oh shit.* "We don't have time to worry about the Patriots right now, Dad. Why don't you stay here and be supportive? Bridger and I are going to go for a drive and see if we can spot the girls."

"Good thinking, will do!" Dave toddled off towards the living room. Joe and Bridger were out the front door like a shot, popping open the doors and clearing the beer cans out of the back of Bridger's minivan.

"Laura, you almost ready?" called Joe as the last of the cans hit the driveway. "We need to get going!"

"All set." Laura came around the side of the house, carrying a large remote control in her hands. Behind her trailed two gleaming silver dinosaurs, about six feet tall, with crystalline blue eyes. Their scaled tails waved delicately behind them as they followed her, scimitar-sharp claws clicking on the pavement.

Joe frowned. "You're bringing the mecha-raptors? Are you sure you can control them this time?"

"Pretty sure. I've done some debugging since the last incident." Laura pressed a few buttons. "Upgraded their auto-pilot, too. So you needn't look so skeptical."

"Yes, dear." Joe shrugged, knowing better than to argue.

"All right, then. Isabelle, Suzette, load up!" The mecha-raptors leaped through the open back gate of the car and coiled themselves up in the cargo area. "Good girls. Take a nap." The cold blue eyes whirred closed. Laura hopped into the back seat behind Joe. "Ready to roll." she said.

With a crunch of crushed cans, the little car pulled out of the driveway and turned east.

It was so dark that Renee could not be sure whether her eyes were open. She registered the feeling of cold, slimy stone against her cheek and the sound of water dripping somewhere. After wiggling her hands and feet to figure out where they were, she slowly pushed herself up off the chilly floor. "Lauren," she whispered. "Lauren, can you hear me?"

"Over here." Renee blindly reached, following the sound of her sister's voice until her fingers found Lauren's shoulder. "Where are we?" the smaller girl asked.

"Beats me. Wherever those guys took us." Renee, her eyes adjusting, found that the darkness was not total; a dim light from somewhere above faintly illuminated a stone-walled room, the corners still in shadow. A heavy oaken door was set flush into one wall, the hinges, and no doubt a stout lock, on the outside.

"Renee," said Lauren. "There's someone else here."

From one of the shadowed corners came a shuffling, stirring sound, accompanied by clanking of iron fetters. "Lauren, get behind me," Renee ordered. "Whatever it is, it's chained."

From out of the gloom, there emerged a hunched, sinewy form, humanlike, moving on hands and knees. Matted hair hung about its head, while shredded rags draped its thin flanks. It shambled forward, to the limit of its chain. "Renee? Lauren?" it wheezed in a voice like a rusty gate. "Princesses, is it really you?"

Renee could scarcely believe her eyes. "Sir Robert? Robert Gronkowski?"

"Yes, yes!" Sir Robert swayed to his feet. "Oh, Princesses, this is all my fault! I was caught by Duke Belichick as I was sending the message to you. He knew you were coming, and he sent his evil minions to ambush you before you could make ready." He staggered, pressing a palm against the wall to keep from falling. "Princesses, I am truly sorry."

"Sit down before you fall down, Sir Robert," said Renee, taking his arm to guide him back down to the floor. "This isn't your fault; we would have come anyway, as soon as we knew that Belichick and Brady were back." She settled him with his back in the angle of the wall. "The question is, what are we going to do now? And also, how on Earth are Belichick and Brady alive again?"

"You are too kind, Princess, entirely too kind." Sir Robert wiped his eyes, composing himself. "It is a fantastic story; I didn't believe it myself, even with the evidence of my own eyes.

"Late last year, just after the Super Bowl, a University of Montana research team disappeared while doing environmental studies at the Berkeley Pit. Their field lab was completely destroyed, and no bodies were ever found, but a few recovered notes make mention of some mysterious creature pulled up in their dredge from the depths of the Pit. I read the news report myself, but I didn't make the connection immediately. Not until one horrible night." Sir Robert shuddered.

"It was late. I was working in the lab, trying to find a way to decrease the power on my hypno drones, the ones that turn people into Patriots fans. They must be decommissioned gradually, as you know, or the shock of sudden withdrawal will cause widespread chaos.

"Suddenly, from the door, I heard the panicked mewing of my kitten, Pickles. Turning round, I saw the figure of Belichick, horribly mutated, but alive, standing there in the shreds of his ratty hoodie with his twisted claws around Pickles' throat." Sir Robert buried his face in his hands. "I could do nothing to resist. With Pickles as hostage, Duke Belichick forced me to increase the power of the hypno drones, and also to engage their replication feature, causing them to make more and more of themselves." He swallowed hard. "He keeps me imprisoned here. Rarely, I am taken out to assist with the deployment of the drones. It has been weeks since I last saw Pickles. I fear that he is lost." Tears filled Sir Robert's eyes.

"And Brady?" Renee prodded. "Last we saw, Lauren had deflated him and stuffed him under a sofa. Are you sure that he's also alive?"

"Alive is an overstatement, Princess, but he exists. Belichick forced me to build an android and program it with Brady's consciousness, which he had saved on a thumb drive some years ago."

"You uploaded his mind into a robot?" The girls goggled.

"Well, in a way. The duke directed that the Brady Bot 3000 be improved in certain respects, so I buried his arrogance and entitlement programming under artificial obedience circuits. He is considerably more docile and agreeable than the original." Sir Robert chewed a ragged thumbnail. "Oh, Princesses, this *is* all my fault. What are we going to do?"

Renee took a deep breath. "First, we're going to get out of this cell. Then, we're going to destroy those hypno drones. After that, we'll see." She produced a bobby pin from her hair. "Give me your hands. Let's start by getting those chains off."

"A toast," said the devil, raising a glass of claret. "To new friends and great endeavors."

"Hear, hear," replied Zeus, lifting his goblet of mead. "And to our gracious host, Duke Belichick, for bringing us all together." He saluted the duke, seated across the round table in the reception room of Foxborough Hall. The duke smiled inside his hood and inclined his head in acknowledgement. Zeus drank deeply, as did the devil and Odin, who swigged from a tankard of beer. Odin's fearsome war hound, Shukir, dozed in a coal-colored heap on the rich carpet at his master's side.

"And may I say, your Excellency, what a fine accommodation you have given us," continued the devil, setting his glass down on the polished table top. "Love what you've done with the place. These chandeliers, for example," he said, indicating the filigreed copper light fixture overhead. "Wherever did you find them?"

The duke laughed, rasping in his throat. "Tommy made those especially for me. Used his optical lasers to carve 'em out, finer than any smith could make. He's got a wonderful eye for design, and he loves to please his old man. Isn't that right, Tommy?" he wheezed, clapping the shoulder of the Brady Bot 3000, which was seated stiffly at the duke's right hand.

"Yes, Father," said the Brady Bot. "It is exactly as you say."

"Indeed it is," agreed the duke, settling into his cushioned chair. To be sure, he thought, he missed the original Tommy, truly he did, but there was no denying that the newer model was so much, well, *easier* to get along with. The duke raised a claw, beckoning a servant. "Another round, gentlemen?"

Odin, shook his head, covering his mug with his hand. "Not for me. Need to keep my wits sharp for when the Koontz boy gets here. *If* he ever does."

"Well, now, dear friends, that is a fair question," replied the devil, looking at the duke. "Duke Belichick assured us that once young Joe realized his nieces had been kidnapped, he would surely come to the rescue, only to find us three waiting for him. Well, the kidnapping is accomplished, here we are waiting, and yet, no Joe. What can be keeping him?"

"Never fear, devil," said the duke. "As I said, Sir Robert got his message to the princesses away before I could stop him, which was unfortunate, but it will also serve as a clue to lead Joe here to Foxborough. And thanks to our mutual assistance, I have the princesses safely stowed, unable to hinder the launch of my hypno drones, while you gentlemen are soon to have your long-awaited revenge."

Zeus grunted in his beard. "It had best be as you say. The Koontz boy has plagued me for years. Did I tell you, he stole the secret of fire from me back in the nineties, and later tricked me into releasing a town I had in my power?"

The devil shook his head. "He's nothing but trouble. He once cheated me of a soul I had bought fair and square, and then made his way to Hell and humiliated me in my own domain."

"He lured a whole herd of woolly mammoths to my house," put in Odin, "and made them shit all over my front yard."

Silence.

"All right then!" said the duke, briskly. "I'm off to oversee the next phase of the hypno drone deployment." He stood, the Brady Bot rising as well. "Gentlemen, please make yourselves at home, and do not hesitate to send a servant to me if you should need anything. Though, of course, from this moment on, I anticipate that there will be no problems."

At that exact moment, three problems and two mecha raptors were pulling up to the edge of the moat around Foxborough Hall in Bridger's battered minivan. "Shit," said Joe. "The drawbridge is up. What now?" On the far side of the moat, the massive oaken bridge stood on end, tipped against its chains; a huge wooden gate just beyond.

Laura, remote control in hands, was limbering up the mecha raptors after their long trip, steel scales sliding over each other as they uncoiled and stretched their limbs. "Can we swim across? Once we get to the other side, I think Isabelle and Suzette can get the gate open."

"I don't think swimming is an option." Joe was using a long stick to probe the noxious glop that filled the moat. As he withdrew the stick, the end smoldered and dripped sizzling droplets that burned the grass.

"Hold up," said Bridger. "I think I can get you across." He lay on his belly, face hanging over the edge of the moat, inches from the surface of the ooze. "Here goes nothing." He bent his head and sipped.

"Bridger, no!" cried Joe.

Bridger lifted his head and gulped, slime running down his chin. "Relax. I still have that iron liver that I got from Odin in exchange for you banishing those mammoths. Nothing can poison me." He dipped his head again and drank.

And drank.

And drank.

He drank the whole moat, right down to the dry bottom. Afterwards, he burped. "I gotta pee," he said.

"You go take care of that," said Laura, fiddling with her remote. "I'll work on getting the hatch open." Bridger toddled off into the woods, while Laura and the mecha raptors jumped down into the empty moat, crossed, and climbed up the other side. "All right, ladies," she said. "Time to shine."

The main gate, closed up tight, was surrounded by openings in the stone wall for archers, each opening having a small ledge facing out. At the touch of a button, both mecha raptors began to ascend the wall, balancing delicately on the ledges. Swiftly and silently, they gained the top, stood for a moment, then dropped over the other side.

Joe climbed up to stand behind Laura, followed by Bridger, back from his pee. He peered over her shoulder to look at the video screen embedded in the controller. "What's going on?"

"Oh, you know, just raptor stuff." Laura was absorbed in the buttons and dials.

"Looks like a lot of blood." The screen was a blur of flashing silver claws and collapsing servants in Foxborough livery.

"Nah, no more than you'd expect." The picture stabilized, and Laura rotated the control, looking for something through the raptors' eyes. "There it is. Main gate latch. Work on it, girls." From inside the door came the scrape of steel teeth on iron, until with a screech the bolts were drawn and the door swung open.

The trio stepped inside. "Excellent girls, lovely girls," said Laura, stroking the mecha raptors' heads. "I'm going to let you off leash for a bit. Go enjoy yourselves." She pushed a red button on the control, and the raptors turned and bounded off, sleek and toothy. "I put them on autopilot," Laura explained. "They can clear the way for us."

"All right, then. Let's go look for Renee and Lauren." Joe led the way forward, through the massive wooden doors.

Inside the doors, they found themselves in the great hall of the fortress. Empty trestle tables and benches crowded the floor, while a high table with ornately carved chairs stood on the far side of the vast space. Stairways and passages radiated out through the stone walls.

"Hey, Joe," said Bridger. "Where'd you get the cat?"

"What cat—oh, hey." Joe looked at the tiny orange kitten, currently clawing its way up his pant leg, in surprise. "Huh, another one. They must just like me."

"I don't know how you manage to find cats wherever we go," said Laura. "Now, come on, focus. We have to find the girls."

"Okie dokie," replied Joe, tickling the kitten under the chin. "Let's go."

"Can you see anything, Lauren?" called Renee, perched on Sir Robert's shoulders.

"Found a hole in the wall. Boost me up a little higher." Up on tiptoe on her sister's outstretched hands, Lauren scrabbled at the stone, feeling for the opening in the stone. "Got it! Wait there and I'll see where this goes." Lauren levered herself into the narrow aperture, sliding forward on her belly.

The shaft was not long, a ventilation duct only piercing the thickness of the wall. Lauren eased forward toward the opposite end, poking her head out into the space above the oaken cell door. Below, she saw a single guard in Patriots livery, parked on a wooden stool with his back against the door, playing Tetris on his phone. This was right in Lauren's wheelhouse. She counted to herself, one, two, three, and then dropped.

From inside the cell, Renee and Sir Robert heard a thud, followed by a short scream that faded into an anguished gargle. Then, silence.

"Lauren?" whispered Renee. "Are you OK?"

"I'm fine," came Lauren's voice. "Hang on, I'm finding his keys. It's kind of a mess." With a squeal of rusty metal, the lock turned and the door swung open, revealing a grinning Lauren and a heap of guard parts. "Watch your step." Renee and Sir Robert stepped out into the corridor.

Suddenly, from the spiral staircase at the end of the hall, there came the echo of multiple footsteps. "Someone's coming!" hissed Renee. "Quickly, find weapons!" She armed herself with the guard's wooden stool, Sir Robert grabbed a flaming torch from the wall. Lauren merely bared her teeth.

From the stair, the footsteps were growing louder. "It's got to be this way, right?" said a man's voice. "Dungeons are always underground." Rounding the last corner, Joe entered the corridor, Laura and Bridger on his heels.

Sir Robert raised his blazing torch like a club. "Die, peasants!"

The orange kitten, riding on Joe's shoulder, mewed in alarm.

Sir Robert lowered his club. "*Pickles!*" He dropped the torch to the floor, where it drowned in a puddle of water. The kitten leaped from Joe's shoulder into the knight's arms and butted his head against Sir Robert's shoulder, purring madly. "Who are you?" the knight demanded. "What were you doing with my cat?"

"They're my family! And Bridger!" Renee cried, flinging herself at them and wrapping her arms around Joe's midsection.

Sir Robert eyed them with suspicion. "Your family, princess?"

"Yes!" Renee grabbed Joe's hand. "Guys, this is our friend, Sir Robert Gronkowski. You've heard of him." Sir Robert drew himself up straight, still a stately figure in spite of his rags.

"Sir Robert, this is my Uncle Joey, his best friend Bridger, and my Aunt Laura."

"My lady." Sir Robert made a courtly bow, his soft brown eyes on Laura's.

"Hi." Laura smiled back, smoothing her hair self-consciously.

"That'll do," said Joe. "Renee, Lauren, follow us. Your mom is worried sick, and we're taking you home."

"But we can't go home now!" cried Renee. "Bill Belichick is going to unleash hypno drones that will turn us all into Patriots fans! We have to stop him!"

Bridger frowned. "Dude, your dad. She's telling the truth."

"I know. Shit." Joe turned back to Renee and Sir Robert. "All right. What do we have to do?"

"The main computer terminal is in the western tower, just under the hover jet pad," said Sir Robert. "If I can get enough time to work on it, I can disable the drones remotely. It will be risky, because many of the current Patriots fans will suddenly be maddened by smugness withdrawal, but I don't see that we have a choice. We must act quickly."

"All right, then, let's go." Joe turned and led the way up the stairs, the group following close behind him.

They emerged into the great hall, which was deserted. "Nobody here," said Joe. "Laura, your mecha raptors do this?"

"I don't think so. No bodies." Laura fiddled with her remote. "Here, I'll turn on the beacon and call them to us."

"Belichick must have all his people on the battlements assisting with the drone deployment. We must hurry, while the coast is clear." said Sir Robert. "The western tower is through here." He led the group through an archway, and up another spiral staircase.

In another part of the castle, before a blazing fireplace, Odin's war dog Shukir suddenly raised his head and wuffed.

"What is it, boy?" asked Odin, half-rising from his repose on a sofa. "Something happening?"

Shukir chuffled again, rising and walking stiffly to the door. His red eyes burned against his coal-black coat.

"What is it?" asked the devil from his chair by the window. He reached out and shook Zeus, who had been dozing in an adjacent recliner. "Stir yourself," he said. "Something's up."

"Show me, Shukir." Odin had also risen, and was crossing the room. Shukir barked once and bounded down the stairs. "Sic 'em, Shukir, good boy!" Odin disappeared after the dog.

The devil and Zeus, passing a glance between them, followed swiftly.

"This way, we're nearly there," said Sir Robert. "Through this passage." The group passed through a short corridor and emerged into the main computer room of Foxborough Hall. It was lit from above by one of the duke's immense copper

252

chandeliers; the walls were lined with blinking, humming supercomputers, fans whirring quietly in the half-light. A chair sat in front of a small hutch on the far side of the room; inside, a blank login screen glowed over an illuminated keyboard. "The main terminal. I'll need several minutes to take the drones offline."

"We'll guard the entrance," said Joe. "Girls, stay on the far side of the room, by Sir Robert. I don't want you getting in the middle of anything." Renee, Lauren, and Laura started across the room. "Not you," said Joe.

"Damn it," said Laura, returning to the entrance.

"I'll hurry." Sir Robert crossed to the terminal, sat, and murmured to the console. *Welcome, Sir Robert*, said an electronic voice. The knight huddled over the keyboard, tapping furiously.

They saw the eyes first, glowing redly in the darkness of the corridor. Gleaming white teeth materialized next, as Shukir emerged from the gloom, hackles raised, glaring at the little group. He threw his head back and howled, an unearthly sound that froze the blood of everyone in the room. The awful sound was still echoing as old man Odin stepped into the room, a soft chuckle rattling inside his ribby chest. "Well, well, what have we here? If it isn't young Joe Koontz, come back for another visit. I shall have to send my welcoming party." His eyes narrowed. "Shukir! Få ham! Get him!"

Shukir roared and leaped. Joe closed his eyes and threw his arms up, wrapped so tightly around his head that he barely heard Bridger cry "Shuki! Hey, buddy, long time no see!"

A soft thud in front of Joe. Slowly, he opened his eyes. Shukir was standing still before him, tail lowered, looking puzzled. He wagged a little, uncertain.

Bridger elbowed Joe out of the way and knelt beside the massive hound. "Joe, you remember Shuki. We had some donuts and went for a nice car ride that one time we got lost in Canada. We're besties. Aren't we, good doggie? Aren't we?" Shukir extended his muzzle towards Bridger, sniffed, and then, with a yelp of recognition, flopped to the ground and rolled onto his broad back to await a tummy rub. Bridger obliged, giving it both hands, as he cooed to the giant beast. "Who's a good pup? Who's a very good boy? Is it you? Is it you? It is!" Shukir paddled his paws happily in the air as his master looked on in disbelief.

A dry laugh came from the direction of the corridor. Looking up, the group saw the devil leaning against the wall, smiling sardonically. "I might have expected as much," he smirked, tapping a cigarette on a silver case. "So hard to find good help." He lit the cigarette with a flame from the tip of his finger, inhaled deeply, and then exhaled, blowing a perfect ring of smoke. "Unless, that is," he smiled again, "you know just where to look." Smoke curled from his nostrils, permeating the air with a thick haze. "Minions of Hell, heed your master! Come here, and do my bidding!" he called into the thickening air.

From the densest smoke came an obscene chittering sound, high-pitched and garbled, as of a thousand distant voices, arguing shrilly. Out of the miasma and into the room poured dozens of tiny black demons and imps, gibbering and capering, filling every corner. Many carried small, sharp pitchforks. All had mouths filled with rows of pointed teeth.

"Seize them, my demons!" cried the devil. "Drag them back to Hell!" The circling goblins closed in, grabbing at feet and snapping at ankles.

In the midst of the heaving throng, Laura recognized a familiar face. "Number 216?" she called. "216, is that you?"

A piercing whistle rang out, and the ring of demons froze, the clamor falling silent. One imp, slightly larger than the others, detached itself from the crowd. It approached Laura, who knelt to its level as it drew near. It said something in Demonese, something that sounded like "*Boss?*"

Laura clapped her hands in delight. "I knew it was you! How good to see you again!" The imp chittered back, patting Laura's hand with a tiny claw. "Yes, yes, I'm fine," she replied. "Well, you know, not *completely* fine." She gestured at the devil, who was staring, gobsmacked. "But you know, as well as can be expected. But enough about me, how are you, 216? Are you enjoying your paid vacations?"

The demon hung its head and burbled. Laura frowned. "No vacations? But it was agreed upon, you each would have two weeks every year." She shot the devil an accusing look. "It was in the contract he signed, as a condition of your return to work. Is he at least honoring the provision for your tea breaks? Fifteen minutes, twice per shift?" The imp shook its head, gibbering in the negative.

Laura slapped her knees. "I suppose he's not contributing to your retirement, either. Well, we know how to deal with a management that can't abide by its contracts, don't we?" The imp chirped. "That's right!" Laura agreed. "Strike!"

The imp turned to the assembled demons, who had been listening closely. "*Strike!*" it cried, waving its claws overhead.

The crowd erupted, chattering and stamping. From out of the gabble emerged a distinct chant: "*Un-ion! Un-ion!*" Tiny placards appeared atop pitchforks waved aloft. The devil's face was crimson, going into purple.

"Oh, for fuck's sake, you guys." Zeus' booming voice drowned out the noise of the picketing demons. "I have to do everything for you. Literally everything." The god of thunder swept into the room, punting a few unlucky demons into the walls.

"Oh, shit," said Joe. "Anyone got something on this guy?" Bridger, still kneeling by Shukir, shrugged. Laura shook her head. "Crap." Joe turned back to face the angry god.

"I'm nearly done!" cried Sir Robert from the terminal. "Just buy me a few more minutes!"

Insectile sparks of electricity were crawling through Zeus' beard. Current arced between his fingertips as his eyes darkened, the storm gathering. "I've been waiting for this for years. Ever since the nineties, when you stole my fire and lost me my bet on the foot race in Missoula." He closed his eyes, lightning writhing over his face. "I bet so much on that race. My wife was so mad at me." He opened his eyes. "And today, my mortal friend, today is the day you pay!" With a deafening crash, he hurled his thunderbolt. Everyone hit the deck.

The smell of burnt ozone filled the room. "Anybody hurt?" called Joe.

"I'm good," said Bridger.

"Me too!" replied Laura.

"We're fine," chimed Renee.

"WHAT THE ACTUAL FUCK?" screamed Zeus, from inside the copper chandelier, which was now on the floor, enclosing him in a metallic cage. "How the fuck are you not dead?" He glowered at Joe, who had sneaked over to the wall during the god's monologue, and who now held a pocket knife in one hand and the severed end of a chandelier rope in the other. Zeus charged another ball of lightning and flung it at Joe's head, only to see it crash into the copper mesh and flow harmlessly to the ground.

"Well done, Joe!" cried Sir Robert, on his knees behind the terminal. "The chandelier is acting as a Faraday cage! He can't get his lightning out!"

Joe blinked. "To be honest, I really didn't think that would work."

Sir Robert hit a final key. "It's done! The drones will be coming offline." He stood. "We should be getting out of here.

There's no telling what the Patriots fans will do once the mind-control is withdrawn."

"Which way?" asked Joe, helping Laura to her feet.

"Through here." Sir Robert indicated another door, in the furthest corner of the computer room. "The hover jets are on top of the tower. We can steal a couple and fly out of here."

"Sounds good."

The group made for the door. As Joe reached out to turn the handle, it flew open, banging into the wall behind. "What the shit," growled Duke Bill Belichick "is going on down here?" The Brady Bot 3000 loomed up behind him.

"Oh, no," moaned Sir Robert. The group retreated as Belichick and the Brady Bot advanced into the room.

"Tommy, my boy," said the duke, a scowl twisting his melted face, "I have had just about enough of this shit. The final hypno drones are almost ready to launch. We don't need him anymore." He pointed a withered claw at Sir Robert. "Fry this son of a bitch."

"Yes, Father." The Brady Bot's eyes brightened, glowing hotter and hotter as its optical lasers charged.

"NO!" Renee pushed in front of Sir Robert. "You're too late! The hypno drones are coming offline right now! You've lost!"

"Liar." The duke's eyes narrowed.

"It's true!" Renee persisted. "You're finished! You'd better run while you still can."

"Father," said the Brady Bot, eyes still glowing. "Father, I hear something outside."

"No!" gasped the duke, running to a surveillance monitor. On the screen, trained on the main gate of Foxborough Hall, people were massing. Some were armed with torches and pitchforks; others were stripping off Patriots gear, flinging it to the ground and stamping on it. Even inside the stone-walled computer room, the growl of the mob was audible, rising moment by moment. "It cannot be!"

"Oh, shit," said Bridger. "I think we left the gate open."

"TOMMY!" the duke shrieked. "Kill them! Kill them all!"

"Yes, Father. I heard you the first time, Father." A small, petulant crease had appeared between the Brady Bot's brows. "There is no need to nag me all the time."

"What did you say?" The duke raised a warning claw. "Are you talking back to me, boy?"

"No, Father." The Brady Bot refocused, lasers whining as they reached full power. "Why would I do that?" A note of sarcasm.

Renee spotted her opening. "That's right, Tommy! Do what your Daddy says!" she jeered.

"Princess, be careful," whispered Sir Robert.

Renee ignored him. "Forget about what you want to do. Forget about going to the mall with Stacy! You can just stay home and work on film review forever, because that's what Daddy's boys do!" The Brady Bot's face twisted, contorted into a hideous grimace. The lasers in its eyes began to dim.

"Tommy," warned the duke. "You do as you're told. You'd better."

"I always do as I'm told." The Brady Bot spoke slowly, through clenched teeth. "I *always* have to do what you tell me, and I *never* get to do what I want, and I *never* get to go to the mall with Stacy and IT IS NOT FAIR!" Its swiveled its head, fixing the duke with icy blue eyes. "Is it–*Daddy?*" With a strangled scream, the Brady Bot lunged, tackling the duke to the ground and gripping him round the throat. The duke struggled and kicked, but he was no match for the furious android.

"To the roof!" shouted Renee. "Hurry!" She led the charge through the door and up the stairs. On the floor, the duke fluttered feebly, still clutching at the Brady Bot's wrists.

Laura brought up the rear. As she reached the door, she was suddenly arrested by a loud whistling scream from the main corridor. She turned, and beheld the mecha raptors, Isabelle and Suzette, crowding the far doorway. The Brady Bot, also distracted, looked up from strangling the duke.

Isabelle and Suzette, for their part, took in the entire scene through the lenses implanted in their crystal eyes. They registered Laura across the room ("FRIEND" blinking onto their optical displays), the downed duke ("NON-THREAT") and finally the Brady Bot, whose clear blue eyes and forward posture exactly matched their own. "RIVAL RAPTOR" flashed across their displays. They screamed again and charged.

Shit, thought Laura. *I really need to improve their species recognition software for the next model.* She closed the door on the sounds of slashing and biting.

The growl of the approaching ex-Patriots rabble grew louder in the computer room. Downstairs, something crashed and broke, and feet tramped on the stairs. By the far wall, the mecha raptors were still working over the Brady Bot 3000.

"I reckon we're about done here," said Odin, his golden spear appearing in his hands at the snap of a finger. "Drop you gents anywhere?"

"I wouldn't mind a lift to Hell, if it's not too far out for your way," said the devil, stomping a demon carrying a sign that read *NO TEA BREAKS, NO TORMENTS.* "Apparently I have some work to do there."

"I'd take a ride to Olympus," put in Zeus, still inside the chandelier. "Also, can you guys help me get out of here?"

"Well, all right." Working together, the devil and Odin lifted the light fixture off the king of the gods. Odin snapped his fingers. "Shukir! Come here!" The dog padded over obediently and sat down beside his master. "I ought to make you walk back to Valhalla, you traitor. Everyone ready?" Odin began to twirl the spear, weaving the golden net. The air wobbled, and the room was empty, save for the prostrate, twitching form of the duke, the two squabbling mecha raptors, and a few pieces of the Brady Bot 3000.

"Oh my God." Renee hung over the battlement, looking down at the main gate of Foxbrough Hall. People were pouring through, more every minute. The muffled roar of their rage drifted up to the top of the tower, along with the smoke of several fires.

"This place won't last long." Sir Robert was putting a hover jet through pre-flight checks. "We need to get out of here, but we won't all fit in one jet. My lady, can you pilot this model?"

"Of course." Laura took the proffered keys and jumped in. Joe and Bridger followed.

Sir Robert jerked open the door of the second hover jet. "Stand by to take off! Quickly, Princesses, into the jet!" he urged, climbing into the pilot's seat, Pickles the kitten cradled in one arm. "We must leave now!" Renee and Lauren leaped in, pulling the door shut behind them.

The engines whirred as they powered up, and, as flames bloomed on the battlements, the jets lifted off. In moments, they were clear.

"Renee." Lauren tugged her sister's sleeve. "Look." She pointed down, towards the tower. A robed figure, hood flapping behind a hairless, shriveled skull, staggered from the open door to the edge of the parapet. Clawing at the air with twisted hands, Duke Bill Belichick opened his mouth in a silent scream. Then the flames rose, the smoke billowed, and he was gone.

The air shimmered above Missoula, Montana, as two hover jets uncloaked, coming in for a landing. They touched down delicately on the front lawn of the girls' house, and the doors whooshed open, silver gangways extending down to the ground.

"Renee! Lauren!" The girls' mother ran out of the house. She knelt down and hugged her daughters. "Where have you been? I was so worried!"

"It's a long story, Mom," said Renee. "But don't worry, we saved the world again. Let's go inside and get some cookies, and we'll tell you all about it."

"Cookies!" Lauren took her mother's other hand, and the three walked up the steps and into their home.

"I guess this is goodbye," said Laura to Sir Robert.

"I fear it is, my lady. The hypno drones were my creation; it is my responsibility to repair the damage they caused." He bowed over her hand. "I must be away." And with that, he climbed back into his hover jet, raised a hand in farewell, and lifted off into the darkening sky, Pickles the kitten in the copilot's seat.

"What'd I miss?" Grandpa Dave had materialized by Joe's side. "Was there an adventure?"

"Kind of," said Joe. "But I think we've got everything sort— Dad, what's that?" He indicated the cardboard box in Dave's hands, piled high with Patriots t-shirts, coffee mugs, and a gigantic red and blue foam finger.

"Oh, just some stuff I'm taking to the dumpster." Dave blinked. "I don't know why; it just came to me that I didn't need them anymore. And then I felt like I wanted to break some stuff. But I'm OK now."

Joe put an arm around Dave's shoulders. "Glad to hear it, Dad. You ready for dinner? I'm thinking pizza."

"Pizza!" Bridger grinned. Arm-in-arm, the friends ambled towards the house. And they lived happily ever after, until the next time.

THE END

54295761R00164

Made in the USA
Columbia, SC
28 March 2019